# FLOWERS GO FLYING IN CRUMBLETON

CRUMBLETON BOOK 2

BETH RAIN

Copyright © 2024 by Beth Rain

Flowers Go Flying in Crumbleton (Crumbleton: Book 2)

First Publication: 7th June, 2024

All rights reserved.

No part of this book may be reproduced in any form or by any electronic or mechanical means, including information storage and retrieval systems. Except for use in any review, the reproduction or utilization of this work, in whole or in part, in any form by any electronic, mechanical or other means now known or hereafter invented, is forbidden without the written permission of the publisher.

Published by Beth Rain. The author may be contacted by email on bethrainauthor@gmail.com

❀ Created with Vellum

# PROLOGUE

## CRUMBLETON TIMES AND ECHO - 14TH JUNE

### What's on This Week

**Bendall's Stores Special Offer!**

The weather is finally due to cheer up at the weekend - perfect timing for Stuart's special offer on bamboo skewers (middle door), fresh sausages (right-hand door) and all flavours of Crumbleton-in-the-Dip Dairy Ice Cream (left-hand door, past the tinned goods and around the back next to the breakfast cereal. Please remember to close the freezer when you've loaded up your basket!)

**Wedding Wonders at the Dolphin and Anchor - Saturday!**

It's the first big bash of the season on Saturday. Wishing luck to our very own Milly Rowlands at *Milly's Flowers* who's in charge of the flowers for the big day.

**A Note on Parking**

A quick reminder to everyone who isn't a hotel resident to move your cars over into the Marsh Carpark to make way for the bride and groom and guests before the big day. Please note - there will be no parking on the grass at the back because the ground is still unseasonably wet from all the rain. The Marsh Carpark is only partially submerged at present - council engineers are working on the problem.

**Caroline Cook. Editor**

CHAPTER 1

MILLY

'Witter-woo boss! Get you… I didn't know you had *actual* legs!'

Milly Rowlands came to an abrupt halt on her way out of the tiny staff bathroom at *Milly's Flowers*. She glared at her trainee. It had precisely zero effect. Jo Burton just stood there with her customary cheeky grin plastered across her face.

'I have legs,' Milly muttered.

'Very nice ones, too!' giggled Jo, wiggling her eyebrows.

'Oh hush!' said Milly. She bit her lip, doing everything she could to keep a stern expression on her face… but as usual, a smile was threatening to break its way through.

This was what always happened whenever Jo was in the shop. The girl might be a complete scatterbrain – and she definitely approached her work with more enthusiasm than care – but she was unerringly cheerful. Almost obnoxiously so. Still, it meant that she was a joy to have around, and every single one of their customers at *Milly's Flowers* adored her.

'Seriously though,' said Milly, 'do I look okay?'

She wasn't really sure why she was bothering to ask Jo. The girl definitely had style – but not the kind Milly was aiming for right now, considering she was off to a very fancy-pants wedding.

This morning, Jo's purple hair had been teased into corkscrew curls. Although she was wearing her *Milly's Flowers* pastel pink polo shirt, she'd pulled it on over a long-sleeved skull and crossbones top. The bottom half of her outfit boasted a lurid pink net tutu over fishnet tights. The whole look was finished off with a pair of floral embroidered Doc Martins.

Milly smirked. She really was going to have to go back over the uniform policy again at some point… but not right now. Jo was doing her a huge favour by stepping in to deal with her Saturday deliveries – including ferrying the wedding flowers down to the Dolphin and Anchor so that Milly could turn up looking like an actual guest, rather than a bedraggled, overworked florist.

'You look great,' said Jo, studying Milly's wrap dress with its white, blue and pink forget-me-not print. 'Give me a spin so I can see the full effect.'

Milly raised one eyebrow but then – realising Jo

wasn't about to let her off the hook – executed a reluctant pirouette.

'It really suits you,' said Jo, nodding her approval. 'I don't think I've ever seen you look so girly!'

'Yeah… well…' said Milly awkwardly.

'It was a compliment,' laughed Jo. 'You know, considering you spend nearly every waking moment talking about weddings, I don't think I've ever known you to go to one before.'

'That's because I'm usually delivering flowers via the back door,' said Milly, ambling over to the large packing table that ran down one side of the shop. She started to survey the array of vases, boxes, bouquets and cartons of fresh blooms that were all waiting to be loaded into the van Jo had just parked outside on the cobbles.

'You get invites all the time, though,' said Jo.

Milly nodded. In fact, she'd received no fewer than half a dozen wedding invitations that week alone.

As the owner of the one and only florist in Crumbleton, Milly spent a high percentage of her working week talking nuptials with over-excited brides-to-be. In fact, if she was forced to put a number on it, she'd bet that well over half her words in any given day were allotted to bouquets, button holes and bridesmaids' posies. Perhaps that was why - when it came to Saturdays - Milly never felt like getting involved in the whole big-white-dress extravaganza.

Nope – Milly didn't usually *do* weddings. She

preferred to keep things strictly business. Deliveries only - and even then, she did her best to nip in the back door, drop off the blooms and then get out of *I Do City* before anyone could spot her. Sure, she was invited to enough of the blasted things to fill every single Saturday until she hit retirement, but cute little girls scattering rose petals and nervous guys with flower-stuffed buttonholes weren't really her thing.

Milly didn't have anything against weddings in particular - after all, they were responsible for a hefty chunk of her livelihood. It was the bit that came after *I Do* that she had a hard time with. The whole idea of pledging her life to one person? Weird. A bit scary. A bit…

'URGH!'

'What?' gasped Jo, nearly dropping the carton of buttonholes she'd just picked up.

'Sorry! Nothing…' said Milly, quickly casting around for an excuse for her involuntary outburst. 'Erm… I thought I saw a spider, that's all.'

'But you're not scared of spiders,' said Jo, narrowing her eyes and cocking her head.

'Or… maybe a bird?' said Milly.

'Riiight…' Jo snorted. 'Gotta watch out for those terrifying robin-tarantulas here in Crumbleton. Seriously, boss, I think the idea of going to a wedding has loosened one of your screws!'

'Oi!' laughed Milly. 'My screws are all fine and

dandy, thank you very much! Now... let's get moving. You start loading while I check this lot over.'

Jo shrugged and headed off to open up the van, ready to receive the day's deliveries. Milly breathed a sigh of relief the minute her trainee disappeared from sight. She just needed two seconds of peace to get her head back on straight.

Drawing the massive bridal bouquet towards her, Milly turned it slowly to make sure it was absolutely perfect. It wasn't *her* kind of thing - but it was exactly what the bride had asked for. Large, bright and impressive had been the three stipulations for the bouquet - and Milly was confident she'd managed to achieve all three. She just hoped the bride had been busy with the dumbbells because the thing weighed an absolute ton! Still, it looked amazing and would be complemented perfectly by the flower girls' bright hoops and the gerbera buttonholes for the men.

'So, what's different about this wedding?' said Jo, bouncing back into the shop.

'What do you mean?' hedged Milly, tweaking a bit of greenery that really didn't need adjusting.

'I mean,' said Jo with exaggerated patience, 'you barely know the bride *or* groom.'

'Do too!' said Milly.

'Go on then,' said Jo, 'what's the bride's name?'

Milly racked her brain, her eyes darting around as she tried to remember. 'Elizabeth!' she said triumphantly.

'You just cheated and looked at the order pad!' snorted Jo.

*Damnit, she couldn't get away with anything!*

'Anyway,' said Jo, 'my point is - why go to this one when you've turned down invitations to about a hundred others?'

'Well... it's local,' said Milly with a shrug. 'I could hardly tell *Elizabeth* that I couldn't manage to make it down as far as the Dolphin and Anchor, could I?'

It was true – the wedding was taking place in the old hotel right at the bottom of Crumbleton's steep hill... but that wasn't the real reason she'd finally broken her self-imposed wedding ban.

'Yeah... I'm not buying it!' said Jo, narrowing her eyes. 'Try again.'

Milly shook her head and let out an exasperated sigh. Jo was right, of course - but there was no way she was about to admit the real reason she'd accepted this particular invitation. If she let it slip that she had the hots for the best man, she'd never hear the end of it!

'You're going all pink,' Jo noted with interest.

'That's because you're stressing me out right now!' growled Milly. 'Get cracking with the loading, will you?'

Jo grinned at her, completely unruffled as she grabbed the bridesmaids' flowery hoops and trotted back outside.

Milly shook her head again, widening her eyes. Thank heavens Jo would be leaving to make a start on the deliveries in just a few minutes. The girl was like a dog with a bone if there was even the slightest scent of impending gossip... and this would *definitely* count as gossip if she let the cat out of the bag.

She'd managed to keep quiet about her crush for months. Eighteen months and counting, in fact. The last thing she needed to do was let his name slip out in front of Miss *Gob-Almighty* Burton!

Part of the problem was that Milly had been single for... well... forever. At least, that's what it felt like. It meant that any hint of a man in her life would definitely get tongues wagging!

It wasn't that she didn't want to find a guy to share her life with... she was just... independent. She liked her space. Plus, there was the unfortunate fact that she tended to attract stage-one clingers for some reason.

Milly hadn't even been on a date for nearly two years. What was the point? If she knew from the beginning that it was only going to amount to a glass of wine or a meal at most before she had to disentangle herself, why bother getting into the mess to start with?

She'd simply never had the good luck to come across someone she could handle being with for more than a couple of months before she wanted to put the brakes on.

Apart from one guy. The one she'd met at a town event eighteen months ago. The one she'd accidentally kissed in the dark carpark of the Dolphin and Anchor... and then never spoken to again.

*Murray Eddington.*

Milly shivered with delight. He was the only person she'd had even the slightest flutter of interest in for ages - the one person she'd even consider breaking her dating dry spell for.

The problem was – the object of her desire had proven to be more than a little bit elusive. Murray lived on an old trawler in the salt marshes that surrounded Crumbleton. According to the careful snooping she'd done after meeting him all those months ago, he was the Marsh Ranger.

Going by the fact that he was seldom seen in town, Milly had a sneaking suspicion that Murray was probably more comfortable in the company of the birds and the elements than actual people. She didn't have an issue with that… but it *did* make getting to know him a bit of a nightmare.

To begin with, she'd been convinced they'd run into each other again before too long. After all, Crumbleton was tiny. As it turned out, though, Milly had only laid eyes on him a handful of times since that night - and it had always been from a distance. She'd still managed to go weak at the knees every single time though - proving that her monster crush was still alive and kicking! With any luck, this wedding might give her the opportunity to do something about it at long last.

Milly had her sights set firmly on the best man… and she couldn't remember ever feeling this nervous!

'Earth to Milly!' said Jo, snapping her fingers in front of her face.

'What's that?' said Milly, blinking in confusion.

'Wow, where were you?' chuckled Jo.

'Back in bed with a cup of coffee instead of going to a wedding!' said Milly promptly, hoping that it might mask her nervous excitement.

'Blimey,' laughed Jo. 'Anyone would think you're off to help de-louse earthworms for the day instead of going to a shindig full of free bubbly and cake!'

'Do earthworms get lice?' said Milly.

'No idea… but gross job, right?' said Jo.

'Erm… yeah,' said Milly.

'Anyway, I was just asking if the bouquet's going in a box or…?' Jo trailed off.

Milly sighed and shook her head. She loved so many things about Jo - her energy, her good humour, and her creativity all made her a promising trainee. She was popular with the customers and great at sales. Her memory for the finer, more technical details of the business however… needed some work.

'We went over this, remember?' said Milly gently.

'Sure… yeah,' said Jo, scratching her nose.

'Okay, let's go again,' said Milly. 'I've done the ribboning already - because it's just at the bottom of the hill - but any further than that, I tend to do it in the back of the van when I get there.'

'Right!' said Jo, nodding. 'Because the ribbons wick

up the water and you don't want a soggy wedding dress.'

'Exactly,' said Milly. *At least something had gone in.* 'So then - we use the short cylinder glass vases with a bit of water in the bottom, and we place them in the cardboard stands for the back of the van. Then...'

'Three sheets of tissue around the bouquet!' said Jo, clicking her fingers.

'By Jove, I think she's got it!' chuckled Milly.

'See - I do listen,' said Jo.

'Yeah... but you know what?' she said, making a snap decision. 'I'm going for a bigger vase for this blighter! It's just going to topple over otherwise.'

'Good call,' said Jo, nodding.

'Seriously Jo,' said Milly, 'brace yourself when you carry this one in.' She couldn't help it. Images of Jo dropping the armful of bright blooms on the way across the hotel carpark had just started flashing in her head.

'You can trust me, you know,' said Jo.

'Yeah - I know,' said Milly with a smile as she rummaged for a larger vase. 'I wouldn't even trust myself with this one – it's super heavy!'

'Just as well you've got my muscles on the job then,' said Jo, flexing a skull-and-crossbones-clad bicep at her. 'You sure you don't want a lift down the hill in the van?'

'Nah – thanks,' said Milly, shaking her head. The last thing she wanted to do was get locked in the van with Jo right now... she was so nervous, she was bound to spill the beans about Murray! 'I'm looking forward to a walk!'

'That's it,' said Jo. 'There's definitely something up with you. Voluntary exercise? Whatever next?!'

'You're fired!' said Milly.

'Yeah, yeah,' said Jo, hefting the bouquet carefully into its new vase. 'So you keep telling me.'

## CHAPTER 2

MURRAY

'Stupid… stupid… stupid suit!' Murray puffed with every uncomfortable flick of his oars.

He was doing his best, but it turned out that rowing a tiny boat through the brackish waters of Crumbleton's salt marshes while wearing a neatly tailored morning suit was a lot trickier than he'd anticipated.

Maybe this was the reason he *never* wore a suit – let alone one with tails. The blasted thing hadn't seen the light of day for well over a decade and, if he had his way, it would be at least twice as long again before it made another appearance.

Unfortunately, he didn't have much choice in the matter right now, though. His usual uniform of shorts and a scruffy tee-shirt wasn't going to cut it. He *was* the best man, after all!

Murray still wasn't quite sure why Philip had asked him to be his best man. Sure, he was on good terms with his old school friend, but the guy definitely had many other – much closer – mates. Josh was the obvious choice. The pair of them had been practically inseparable for years. They played football together, did the whole Friday night at the pub thing, and had even gone on holiday with various girlfriend combinations over the years. As far as Murray knew, the bride liked Josh too… whereas *he'd* never even met the woman.

Before accepting, Murray had tentatively suggested Josh as a more suitable candidate for the role. Philip had gone very quiet and then – after a pregnant pause - he'd simply repeated his request in a louder voice.

When someone bellowed "WILL YOU BE MY BEST MAN OR NOT?" at you, you couldn't really say *no,* could you? Besides – Murray had never been a best man before - and he was a big fan of giving things a go at least once if the opportunity presented itself.

*Like kissing a beautiful stranger in a dark hotel carpark!*

A huge grin appeared on Murray's face. He knew he probably looked like a total weirdo right now, but there was no one around to judge him other than a heron… and she was more interested in hunting for tasty morsels in the murky water than paying any attention to what his soppy face was doing.

Murray let out a long sigh. As random experiences went, his stolen kiss with Crumbleton's beautiful florist was *definitely* one of his favourites. It had happened well over a year ago now – but it still popped into his head at least once a day.

*Who was he kidding? At least once every hour was more like it!*

It had just been so completely unexpected. He'd ducked out of a decidedly stuffy town planning event at the Dolphin and Anchor for a breath of fresh air, only to discover that she'd had exactly the same idea. He'd barely had the chance to say hello before she'd turned to him and pulled him into a hard, desperate kiss – a kiss that had haunted him ever since.

Murray gave a wriggle of excitement and pulled on the oars a bit harder than his straining suit could handle. There was an ominous ripping sound from somewhere around the back.

'Oops,' he muttered, carefully shortening his strokes again, doing his best to ignore the fact that his heart was hammering, and his hands were starting to feel clammy with nervous excitement. Not only was he heading back to the scene of the kiss… he was finally going to get the chance to speak to the woman who'd taken up residence in his head!

As much as Murray adored living in a grounded trawler on Crumbleton's salt marshes - surrounded by frogs and birds, peace and quiet – there *were* a couple of drawbacks. Having to row everywhere was one of them. The other was the fact that he got very little opportunity to bump into anyone "by accident." By "anyone", he meant Milly Rowlands, of course.

After that wonderful, insane, unexpected kiss – she'd slipped back inside the hotel without a single word… and Murray had been wishing for the chance to get to know her ever since.

He'd certainly made a few more visits to town over the last eighteen months than were strictly necessary… not that any of them had achieved much other than making him feel like a total idiot.

The one time he'd managed to summon the courage to go to her shop with the sole purpose of introducing himself properly, he'd been bounced at by a purple-haired whirlwind who'd informed him that Milly was out doing deliveries. Murray had promptly bought a random bunch of purple irises as an excuse for going in, and then skulked away, feeling like a total fool. That day, he'd made himself a promise that he'd forget the whole thing.

A promise he'd failed to keep.

Spectacularly.

Today – at long last – they were both going to be in the same place at the same time again… and he had every intention of saying hello.

He couldn't make too much of a plonker out of himself at a wedding, could he?

'Other than the fact that you're rowing across the marshes in a suit!' he muttered. That counted as pretty plonker-worthy!

He really should have waited to get changed at the

Dolphin and Anchor, but he hadn't wanted to let the side down by turning up wearing his usual dragged-through-a-hedge-backwards look. There were bound to be guests milling around everywhere, and he didn't want to give a bad impression. He didn't go to many weddings – but even *he* knew that no one wanted an animated scarecrow wandering around, frightening the guests.

If he was being completely honest, Murray didn't really know how the whole event was meant to pan out. Other than keeping an eye on the groom so that he didn't scarper before the "I Do" part of proceedings, he wasn't sure what else there was to his role. He *did* want to get it right, though.

Come to think of it, in this case, "getting it right" might have included staying at the hotel the night before the wedding rather than still being stuck in the boat with less than an hour to go before the ceremony was due to start.

Murray promptly did his best to speed up a bit, and then let out a frustrated huff as the jacket's sleeves threatened to strangle his biceps. At this rate, it was going to take forever to reach the stone wharf near Crumbleton's City Gates.

Okay – it was time to take the bloomin' thing off. He should have done it ages ago... but he hadn't wanted to risk splashing himself with stinky marsh water in the process!

Resting the oars carefully down, Murray wriggled

around, trying to ease his way out of the ridiculous thing without dunking one of the tails overboard in the process.

'Come on, come on, come on!' he muttered.

Great. Now he was half-in and half-out of the jacket... and he had a nasty feeling he was stuck. Doing his best to squash the desire to rip it off and toss the whole thing overboard, Murray let out a frustrated growl... and then jumped when the jacket growled right back at him.

'What the actual...?' he gasped, grabbing onto the edge of the boat as it rocked precariously beneath him.

The hunting heron launched into the sky in a flurry of wings and water droplets, clearly startled by his sudden shout. For a brief moment, Murray wished he could follow her. Instead, he started to pat the twisted mess of seams, lining and pockets, searching for his mobile phone – which was still vibrating somewhere inside the jacket. The minute he managed to free it, Murray glanced at the screen and let out a groan.

'Josh,' he sighed. *Again.*

This had been the biggest drawback of agreeing to Philip's best man request. Josh had been calling him pretty much solidly ever since. Murray might not know what was going on between the two friends, but Josh had made it more than clear that he wasn't happy Murray had stolen his thunder.

Every single time he called, he'd offered suggestions for the best man speech - jokes that would have Philip on his knees with embarrassment, and hints as to why the bride was "settling."

Murray had done his best to ignore it all – including Josh's regular reminder that he was bound to make a total hash of things, but not to worry because Josh would be waiting in the wings to save the day.

'Josh,' he muttered as he answered the call. 'What do you want?'

'What crawled up your butt, grumpy pants?' came Josh's greeting.

Murray bit his lip. The temptation to answer "you" was almost unbearable.

'Erm… this isn't a good time,' he said instead.

'Right, right… because you've finally realised that I'm the right person for the job?' said Josh. 'I'm guessing you've decided not to turn up? See – I told Philip you were completely unreliable. This was bound to happen… the minute he asked someone who lives in a flippin' boat-'

'I thought you and Philip weren't talking?' said Murray, not sure whether to be amused at Josh's total desperation about something as trivial as being asked to be best man, or annoyed because the guy was such a total prat.

'We're talking,' huffed Josh. 'I mean… he's been really busy, so it's been mostly via messages and I've left some on his landline too. I just think he deserves to know that I'm the right guy for the job, that's all. As his *best friend!*'

Murray smirked. He could only imagine the *hundreds* of voicemails Philip had been treated to if his own almost-nightly calls from Josh were anything to go by.

'Anyway,' said Josh, 'it's obvious you aren't going to make it. I'll deal with the flower delivery and I've got a speech prepared because I just knew something like this was going to happ—'

'Don't bother,' said Murray easily. 'I'm on my way right now.'

'No one wants you here!' squeaked Josh.

Murray almost dropped his phone in amusement. 'Weird how they invited me, then,' he chuckled. 'Anyway, Josh, gotta dash... I've got a wedding to get to.'

Murray promptly hung up.

Was missing out on the "honour" of being the best man really enough to reduce a grown man to a bitchy, quivering wreck – or was he missing something here?

He mulled it over for all of three seconds before shrugging. He really couldn't care less. Whatever drama was afoot, Murray wasn't interested. Josh might want him to turn tail and head home, but there was no way he was about to give the weird little weasel what he wanted. For one thing, he wouldn't dream of letting Philip down this close to the big event. For another... he'd waited for a seriously long time for the chance to officially meet Milly Rowlands.

Just the thought of her spurred Murray into action

and less than a minute later, he'd freed himself from his straitjacket and was pulling on the oars again – guiding the boat towards Crumbleton's stone wharf with easy, powerful movements.

## CHAPTER 3

MILLY

'Blimey!' muttered Milly as she ambled into the carpark at the back of the Dolphin and Anchor.

It was jam-packed – both with wedding guests and cars. She definitely recognised a few of them. Clearly, the plea in the Crumbleton Times hadn't done much to get people to shift their vehicles out of the way for the big day. Every single space was full – including the shady one in the corner beneath the conker tree, where a bored-looking horse was dozing at the front of a very fancy carriage.

Milly let out a sigh of relief that she didn't have to navigate this lot with her flower van. It took all of two seconds for the relief to morph into guilt - skiving off to ogle Murray meant the unenviable task had fallen to Jo instead.

Milly had already spotted her trainee parked up on

the cobbles out the front of the hotel – hazards flashing as she hauled the delivery in through the front doors. It was the opposite of what Milly had asked her to do – but given the circumstances, there was no way she was about to complain!

'Hello you!'

Milly whirled around, only to find Caroline Cook grinning at her.

'I didn't know you were coming!' said Milly with a broad smile.

'Like I'd miss the chance for a scoop,' said Caroline, leaning in to give her a hug.

'A scoop at a wedding?' said Milly, frowning at her friend in amusement. She might be the editor for the Crumbleton Times and Echo, but surely even Caroline would struggle to find a juicy story amongst the corsets and corsages!

'You never know,' said Caroline, wiggling her eyebrows. 'Anyway – who am I to say no to free fizz and cake under the guise of work?'

'Jo said almost exactly the same thing earlier,' said Milly.

'Is that trouble-maker here too?' said Caroline, glancing around.

'Only to deliver the flowers so that I wouldn't have to,' said Milly.

'You trusted her with that?' said Caroline in surprise.

'Yep,' Milly nodded. 'Especially as it means I get to

rock up without getting covered in stinky flower water first.'

Caroline narrowed her eyes at Milly. 'You look very nice,' she said slowly. It sounded more like an accusation than a compliment – her words laced with suspicion.

Milly bit her lip. There was no way she was going to tell Caroline the real reason she was here… but her friend knew her far too well.

'What *exactly* are you doing here?' she continued.

Milly snorted – her over-the-top amusement designed to throw Caroline off the scent. 'Erm… celebrating a joyous union between…' she trailed off. Damnit – she'd forgotten the bride's name again, and this time there was no convenient order pad nearby.

'Between?' said Caroline, amusement sparkling in her eyes.

'Two people?' said Milly.

'Who're called…?'

'Mr and *almost* Missus… Davies?' she guessed.

'Try again!' hooted Caroline. 'It's Williams.'

'So close,' huffed Milly. 'Anyway, I did the flowers and the bride asked me. I couldn't exactly turn her down, could I?!'

'Why not?' said Caroline in surprise. 'That's what you usually do.'

'Yeah – but this time the wedding is literally just down the hill from the shop,' said Milly.

This time, she'd had a crush on the best man forever... not that she was going to tell Caroline that.

'I didn't want to be rude!' she added.

'But-'

'Sorry - hold that thought!' said Milly as she felt her mobile phone vibrate in her pocket with an incoming message. She quickly fished it out and glanced at the screen. Having let Jo loose on the deliveries, she didn't want to risk missing an SOS call.

Sure enough, the message was from Jo – but there wasn't any kind of emergency afoot that might save her from Caroline's interrogation.

'Everything okay?' said her friend.

'Yeah,' said Milly, raising an eyebrow in surprise. 'It's just Jo letting me know she's finished delivering the flowers.'

'Blimey – cutting it a bit fine, aren't you?' said Caroline. 'I mean – the bride's probably dressed and ready to go by this point!'

'I did the flowers for the room yesterday,' said Milly with a shrug. 'It's just the bouquet and the bits and bobs for the men and the flower girls. It was the best way to make sure they were fresh and didn't get damaged before the ceremony.'

'Fairy snuff,' said Caroline.

'Listen to this, though,' said Milly, still staring at the text.

*"Flowers delivered. All fine though had to use the front door.*

*Heads up - best man is a total douche. Felt like flobbing in his hip flask"*

Caroline snorted. 'Now that's the kind of customer service everyone deserves.'

'Yeah – but what about the bit about him being a douche…' muttered Milly.

'What about it?' said Caroline with a shrug. 'Being a best man doesn't automatically make him a good guy, you know. There isn't an entrance exam. Wait… do you know the best man?'

Milly paused for a beat. *Did she?!*

'No,' she said. 'No, I don't.'

After all, it wasn't *really* a lie. She'd met him once, and then glimpsed him in the distance a handful of times since. So… she *might* have pounced on him – in this very carpark in fact – but she'd barely spoken two words to him! That didn't count as *knowing* him, did it?

A strange feeling of hollow disappointment seemed to be swirling in her stomach. She'd been so sure that Murray was one of the good guys - that he was a fairytale waiting to happen if only she could summon the courage to do something about it. But…

'Why do you look like someone's just pooped on your pansies?' said Caroline curiously.

Milly shrugged, quickly casting around for an excuse for her sudden change in mood. 'Just trying to decide how I'm going to discipline Jo for this,' she said, waving her mobile – the text still visible on the screen.

'Are you kidding me?' said Caroline in surprise. 'If she's managed to deal with an obnoxious bloke on a wedding-fuelled power trip without any kind of retaliation, the girl deserves praise for her restraint. Not sure I'd manage to do the same!'

'Thank heavens you don't work in customer service,' said Milly, glancing at the text again.

'I'll second that,' said Caroline with a nod. 'Look – they're calling everyone inside.'

Sure enough, the silvery tinkling of a handbell being tortured by a toddler in a suit echoed across the carpark.

'Time to get this show on the road!' said Caroline, offering Milly her arm. 'May I escort you?'

Milly hesitated for a brief second and then grabbed Caroline's elbow with a sense of resignation. It was just as well her friend was there - without Caroline towing her in the direction of the impending nuptials, Milly would have chosen that exact moment to skip out on the whole thing.

The ceremony was mercifully short – and Milly was chuffed to note that the flowers looked perfect. Everything had gone smoothly - with the *I Dos* happening in all the right places, accompanied by a few elegant tears (from the mother of the bride) and a giggle or two (courtesy of the hilarious celebrant who'd definitely missed her calling as a stand-up comedian.)

The only thing Milly found disappointing about the whole affair was the fact that Murray had kept his back to the guests for most of the ceremony. It was a *very* nice back though.

'Well... that's that then!' said Caroline as they stood watching the newlyweds disappear from the room.

'What's next?' said Milly, looking slightly distracted as she craned her neck, trying to catch sight of Murray through the forest of feathered fascinators that had reared up around her.

'Ladies and gentlemen,' came the celebrant's voice. 'Mr and Mrs Williams would like to ask you all to join them back outside for the tossing of the bouquet!'

'That answers that, then,' said Caroline, grabbing Milly's hand and towing her towards the doors. 'Come on – let's get out there for the scrum!'

Milly shrugged and followed her friend... not that she had *any* intention of trying to catch the flying flowers. After all, she knew how much they weighed.

'Why on earth is she so keen to get rid of her bouquet, do you think?' puffed Milly, doing her best to keep up. 'Surely that usually happens after food, and toasts... and bad dancing?!'

'You tell me,' said Caroline. 'You made the thing. Did you spray it with stink-powder or something?'

'No! As if I'd-'

'Chillax, Mills,' chuckled Caroline. 'I was joking! I

think they just wanted an excuse to get everyone outside so that they can get the room ready for the reception and get the disco set up in the corner.'

'Oh!' said Milly. 'Is she really going to throw the flowers in the carpark? What about the gardens... surely that would be a better photo op?'

'According to Kendra, the grass is too soggy after all the rain,' said Caroline as they emerged back into the sun-drenched carpark. 'They didn't want to spend the rest of the day rescuing all the stiletto-wearers from ankle-deep mud.'

'Well, that's fair enough,' laughed Milly. 'Not much space out here for it though, is there?' she added, squeezing down the side of a battered old Volvo. It was going to be tough to find a spot in the crowd where she wouldn't be in danger of getting elbowed in the ribs.

On the other side of the carpark, near the snoozing horse, a gaggle of eager-looking women were already gathering, jockeying for elbow room as they prepared to fight for the bridal bouquet.

'Get over there Mills!' said Caroline, giving her a gentle shove.

'No chance,' spluttered Milly, doing her best to stand her ground in the thickening crowd. 'What about you?'

'No way!' said Caroline. 'Perks of being a reporter – I *observe*.'

Milly giggled as Caroline pulled herself up to her full height and did her best to look haughty and aloof.

'Hope they get on with it, though – I could do with a glass of fizz,' she added, completely ruining the effect. 'Weddings make me thirsty.'

'Mmm,' Milly mumbled her vague agreement as she glanced around, trying to spot Murray in the throng. He had to be out there somewhere, didn't he? She couldn't see him – but then, she couldn't really see much in this chaos.

There wasn't room to swing a cat in the packed carpark. People kept stepping on Milly's toes, and the photographer was busy making things worse by squeezing her way through the crowd – elbows first – clearly intent on reaching the action before she missed the photo opportunity completely.

'Here we go!' said Caroline, nudging Milly and pointing at the bride as she appeared bearing the bouquet. With some difficulty, she raised the flowers over her head and turned her back on the group of jostling women.

As the flowers sailed up into the sky, everything started to move in slow motion – or at least, that was what it felt like to Milly. It wasn't a bad throw at all, considering the weight of the blooms and the fact that the bride's movements were hampered by her bejewelled corset. Her eyes followed the bouquet as it flew in a high arc above the forest of waiting arms.

Then – out of nowhere – someone made a brave leap for the bouquet. The jump was worthy of the Olympics – but the woman's fingers only just managed to clip the stems, sending the flowers spinning wildly in a different direction.

The horse tossed its head nervously.

There was a collective gasp.

A dull thud.

And then - complete silence.

It took a few beats before time sped back up again – but when it did, all hell broke loose.

'Is there a doctor here? Do we have a doctor in the crowd?' shrieked a woman's voice. She sounded more than a little bit hysterical.

'What just happened?' gasped Milly, craning her neck as she tried to work it out. 'Did the horse get loose? Is someone hurt?!'

'Two secs,' said Caroline, scurrying forward, 'I'll find out.'

Milly stared around, looking for Murray again – but before she had any luck, Caroline was back at her side.

'Nothing to do with the horse,' she said, wide-eyed and looking like she was torn between absolute horror and the desire to giggle. 'Your flowers just clonked someone right on the head!'

'Uh oh!' said Milly with a guilty wince. 'Are they okay?'

'The flowers look fine,' said Caroline.

'Not the flowers, idiot,' hissed Milly, 'the person they hit!'

'I shouldn't think so,' Caroline said, shaking her head.

'What do you mean?!' said Milly with a sinking sensation.

'The poor bloke's out cold!'

## CHAPTER 4

MURRAY

Murray was quickly coming to the conclusion that weddings were very stressful things indeed.

Even though he hadn't been entirely sure about the whole thing when he'd accepted Philip's request to be best man, he'd comforted himself with one thought – *how hard could it be?*

As it turned out? Very! Of course, Josh wasn't helping matters one little bit.

Murray had tied his boat up at the wharf next to the shabby old craft owned by the council that that was rarely ever used, and then practically jogged to the hotel. By the time he arrived at the Dolphin and Anchor, the best-man-wannabe had already managed to reduce one of the flower-girls to tears. He'd also upset the catering staff so much that Murray would bet anything Josh's sorbet would have a high concentration of added spit by the time it was served.

Murray had barely had the chance to greet the groom before Philip sent him in search of Josh - with orders to make sure he didn't cause any more drama before the ceremony. He'd only just managed to track him down, and by the look of things, Josh was in serious danger of having his eyes gouged out by the purple-haired whirlwind who'd turned up to deliver the flowers.

Judging by the pure venom pouring from the trainee florist's eyes, Murray was pretty sure she was more than capable of tearing Josh limb from limb… and enjoy the experience while she was at it. If it wasn't for the fact that he had a bit of an ulterior motive, he'd have left the idiot to his fate. This was too good an opportunity to waste, though.

'Josh, you're needed inside,' he said.

Josh didn't even turn around, he was too busy ranting with his face pressed right up against the van window.

Murray let out an exasperated sigh. Striding forwards, he grabbed Josh by the scruff of the neck and dragged him away from the van.

'What the…?' Josh was practically frothing at the mouth, looking slightly unhinged.

'Philip's looking for you!' said Murray, quickly inventing an excuse to get the idiot as far away from the irate girl inside the van as possible.

The magic words worked a treat, and Josh disappeared in a swish of self-importance, his ridiculous top hat tucked under one arm.

'Cheers for that,' breathed the girl. Her venomous scowl turned into a grateful grin as she wound the window down to talk to him. 'I was just wondering whether headbutting him would count as unprofessional conduct. Might have still been worth it anyway!'

Murray grinned at her.

'You're not going to have a go at me for stopping here at the front instead of trying to get into the carpark too, are you?' she added.

'No chance!' said Murray, holding his hands up in a gesture of surrender. 'For one thing, I don't want you to headbutt me, and for another - you'd never get into the carpark even if you wanted to.'

'That's what I told shorty arsy grumpface,' she muttered. 'Then he turned rabid and...' she paused. 'Sorry... he's probably a friend of yours.'

'Nope,' said Murray mildly. 'Definitely no friend of mine.'

'Who asks an idiot like that to be their best man anyway?' she said, looking perplexed.

'No one in their right mind,' chuckled Murray. 'Who told you *he's* best man?'

'He did,' huffed the girl. 'About eleventy-billion times. Talk about a tiny man on a power trip. Anyway – I'd better get going.'

'Two secs,' said Murray quickly, 'is Milly not coming?'

*Damn... did he really have to sound quite so desperate?!*

'She's here,' said the girl, watching him closely, as though she sensed gossip in the air. 'She decided to walk down. Didn't want to get her dress messed up. I saw her go around the back of the hotel a few minutes before that git turned up. Why? Who're you?'

Murray glanced towards the entrance of the carpark and a flutter of nerves ran through him. 'Me?' he said distractedly. 'I'm no one. The... erm... the bride... was asking for Milly,' he added, the fib escaping before he could stop it.

*He really had to stop doing that! Still, it was worth it – Milly was here!*

'Okay Mr No One,' said the girl. 'Do you want me to text Milly and let her know?'

Murray widened his eyes in horror. 'No... no need!' he spluttered. 'I'll... erm... I'll deal with it!'

'Okay, cool!' she said, shooting him a cheeky grin. 'Right, I'd better dash. People to see! Flowers to deliver!'

Before Murray could say another word, he found himself staring at the back of the little pink van as it lurched away across the cobbles.

*Well... she was a character!*

As he watched the van disappear off towards the City Gates, Murray took a deep breath and willed his nerves to calm down. He had a feeling the sudden fluttering in his chest had nothing to do with his impending best man duties – and everything to do with the fact that at some point in the next few hours, he was finally going to *officially* meet Milly. *If* he didn't wimp out, of course.

But first… he'd better go and save Philip from Josh's less-than-tender ministrations… and perhaps find a convenient broom cupboard to lock the idiot in until after the ceremony.

Stealing himself, Murray let out a long sigh before heading back into the bar of the hotel. All he really wanted to do was join the rest of the guests. He'd love to grab a glass of bubbly, wander around admiring everyone's ridiculous headwear, and work on summoning up a bit of courage before chatting up the woman who'd plagued his dreams for a full year and a half. Instead, he had to make sure there weren't any further Josh-shaped disasters brewing.

'Murray… got a sec?'

Kendra collared him just as he was heading through the bar.

'Everything okay?' he asked with a decided sinking sensation.

Kendra nodded and shrugged at the same time. The young barmaid was dressed in smart black trousers and a white blouse. She'd clearly been roped in as an extra waitress for the reception.

'Yeah,' she said hesitantly. 'Chef just asked me to

check with someone... are they really only giving the guests ten minutes to eat each course?'

Murray smirked and nodded. 'That's right.'

'Weird!' she whispered.

'I know!' Murray whispered back.

'I'll let Chef know. He's going to be maaaad!' she said, with a quick smile. 'Thanks, Murray.' She turned and disappeared off towards the kitchen again.

Murray shook his head. He couldn't blame the chef for double-checking. This wedding was shaping up to be weird through and through.

For starters, the happy couple didn't want the ceremony to drag on for too long... or the speeches... or anything, for that matter. It was all about romance against the clock.

The entire day was on a tight timetable just so that the new Mr and Mrs Williams could make the most of the discounted flights they'd got their hands on for the honeymoon. Not that there was anything *wrong* with that... but it seemed a shame to sprint through what was meant to be the most romantic day of their lives just for the sake of saving twenty-quid!

Frankly, Murray couldn't quite fathom their logic... but then he wasn't the one getting married. He was just the guy who'd been put in charge of a stopwatch and told to make sure the entire thing was timed with military precision.

'Okay,' said Elizabeth, dropping her new husband's hand the moment they were out of sight of the cooing crowd. 'That's got that bit out of the way!'

Murray bit his tongue to stop himself from letting out a snort of surprised laughter. That had to go down as one of the least romantic sentences *ever* to be uttered by a newlywed - in the history of forever.

The bride turned to him with narrowed eyes, and he flinched.

'We've got five minutes to throw these!' she hissed, thrusting her massive bouquet under his nose. 'Get everyone out there pronto. As soon as that's done, I need them all in their seats and ready to eat in under ten minutes. GO! GO! GO!'

Murray sprang away from her and shot Philip a look of pure pity – only to find him gazing at his bride in total adoration. The man was either mad... or drugged? Either way, *he* was going to get out of there before Bridezilla could say anything else.

He started to usher a couple of befuddled-looking guests towards the back of the hotel. If he was lucky, maybe he'd bump into Milly out there. He'd love to say hello before the meal kicked off. If his mounting nerves were anything to go by, there was a good chance he might make a bit of a prat out of himself - and he'd prefer to get it over and done with outside, where people were less likely to overhear him placing his foot firmly in his mouth.

Murray had nearly caused chaos during the

ceremony as it was. Just as he'd reached out to hand over Philip's wedding band for the "with this ring, I thee wed" part of proceedings, he'd caught sight of Milly in the crowd. He'd promptly fumbled with the ring on its ridiculously slippery satin pillow - and disaster had only been averted when the celebrant had miraculously caught the glinting golden band in mid-flight.

After narrowly avoiding the embarrassing prospect of asking the entire congregation to get down on their hands and knees to search for a missing wedding ring, Murray had kept his back turned on them for the rest of the ceremony. He couldn't afford to risk catching sight of Milly's smile again. Heavens only knew what he'd do next!

As he stepped through the doors into the busy carpark, Murray took a deep breath of fresh air. Good. There were enough people out there already that he clearly wasn't needed for a few seconds. He'd find a convenient spot to gather his wits - maybe somewhere over near the horse and carriage.

Murray skirted around the edge of the gathering crowd, making his way towards the shady patch where the horse stood with its eyes half-closed, ignoring the goings on around it with an air of admirable boredom.

Murray came to a halt just beyond a cluster of eager-looking women who were busy rolling up their sleeves – making sure their elbows were at the ready. He scanned their faces, searching for one in particular.

Milly wasn't amongst them... but then, considering she'd *made* the bouquet, he couldn't imagine she'd want to take it home with her at the end of the day.

*Where was she, though...?*

Maybe it would be a better idea to focus on the task at hand, rather than ramping his nerves up even further. It wasn't too long before he'd have to make his speech – and he'd been ordered to keep it under three minutes! He'd managed to cut it down to just two jokes, and a toast to the happy couple. If only he could remember the punchline to the second joke, he should be fine.

The problem was... it kept slipping his mind! It had something to do with a penguin... and a dragon? Or was it an armadillo...?

*Damnit, he was going to have to check his notes again!*

Murray fumbled in his pocket, and his fingers had just found the soft edges of his dog-eared speech when the gentle mutterings around him rose in volume.

Glancing up, he spotted Elizabeth yanking impatiently at the skirts of her big, white dress so that she could take up her position with her back to the group of waiting women – who were now screeching with excitement.

Murray watched as she raised the huge bunch of flowers in the air... and they started to fly. Distracted by the cheers from the rest of the crowd, his eyes swept over them, searching for Milly once again.

Suddenly, the sun went in and he shivered. Typical

timing for it to cloud over! He glanced up at the sky in irritation - only to spot something huge heading straight for him.

*That certainly wasn't a cloud.*

It was a bunch of bright sunflowers, roses and gerberas – large enough to obscure the sun.

Murray didn't even think about ducking – there simply wasn't time. He had just started to wonder exactly how much this was going to hurt… when everything went black.

## CHAPTER 5

MILLY

Milly quickly decided it was probably best if she just stayed out of the way. She'd taken a first aid course at school… but she couldn't remember much about it other than lots of giggling when it came to doing mouth-to-mouth on the CPR dummy. Somehow, she couldn't imagine she'd be much help right now.

Besides… she was a florist, not a doctor.

A florist who was currently feeling ridiculously guilty about the poor bloke who'd just received a faceful of *Milly's Flowers'* finest.

There was a tight knot of guests crowded around the spot where the drama had taken place – though Milly had a feeling *they* weren't doing much to help the casualty either. In fact, the majority of them had their mobile phones raised in the air, intent on capturing everything.

*Whatever everything was!* Milly shuddered. She wasn't really sure she wanted to know.

From the half-horrified, half-delighted murmurs that kept drifting her way, it sounded like there was a lot of blood involved... and several missing teeth. Milly had her fingers crossed that this was just a really bad case of Chinese Whispers. Yes – it *was* a big bouquet, and yes – it *was* very heavy, but surely it couldn't have caused any serious damage... could it? Even if the bouquet *had* fallen on him from a pretty impressive height - blood and missing teeth seemed to be a bit far-fetched.

At least... she was busy praying that was the case!

'You okay?' said Caroline, staring at Milly as she shifted guiltily on the spot.

Milly forced herself to stand still for a second. She'd been alternating between craning her neck to see what was happening, and – more importantly, who it was happening to – and then turning sharply away because she didn't really *want* to see anything. She wasn't very good with blood.

Judging by the look of concern Caroline was now giving her, Milly could only assume that her grossed-out expression and weird movements were making it look a bit like she was having some kind of fit.

'Mills, answer me,' said Caroline gently. 'What's wrong?'

'Nothing – I'm fine,' said Milly, scrunching up her face. 'Just wondering who got hurt, that's all.'

## FLOWERS GO FLYING IN CRUMBLETON

'Stay here - I'll go and find out,' said Caroline. 'I want to take some notes anyway... and get some eyewitness accounts while they're still fresh!'

'Hey!' gasped Milly, grabbing her friend's wrist. 'You're not going to put this bit in the paper, are you?'

'Are you kidding me?' laughed Caroline. 'Of course I am! This wedding just earned itself an upgrade. It might even make the front page if the photographer managed to get a decent action shot of the whole thing going down. I'll need a quote from you too, Mills – about the flowers. It'll be great publicity, you'll see!'

As she watched Caroline force her way through the gawking crowd again, Milly let out a low groan. She swayed slightly and wrapped her arms around herself. She was starting to feel a bit odd – weak and a bit wibbly around the edges. Maybe she was in shock or something.

Milly was half-tempted to go and hunt for Murray. She didn't know why – but she had a feeling he'd make her feel better. Perhaps he'd offer to lend her his jacket... or maybe even give her a hug!

Closing her eyes for a brief second, Milly imagined his warm arms closing around her. She shivered. Yep – that would definitely make her feel better!

But then again... perhaps she'd better not. For one thing, Murray might not even remember her – and she was in no fit state right now to remind him about their kiss! For another thing, Murray was the best man. He was probably caught up in the thick of things, dealing with the casualty and making sure the poor guy didn't get trampled.

Blowing out a long breath, Milly glanced over at the crowd again. It seemed to be thinning a bit as people got bored and started to wander back towards the hotel. She still couldn't see the man on the ground, but someone was leading the sleepy horse towards the out-of-bounds gardens – the vintage carriage trundling along behind it.

'What's happening?' said Milly as Caroline reappeared at her side.

'There's an ambulance on its way, so they're moving the horse so that it doesn't freak out and cause any extra havoc!' said Caroline.

'An ambulance?' said Milly, her eyes widening in horror. 'Isn't that overkill? I mean… it was *just* a bunch of flowers.'

Caroline shrugged. 'The guy's still unconscious… so I guess it's the only option.'

'What?' gasped Milly. *That must have been one serious clonk on the head!* 'Who is it?'

'It's the best man,' said Caroline. 'That tall bloke who lives out on the marshes in that old boat.' She paused and clicked her fingers. 'I can't remember his name. I'll need it for the article…'

'Murray,' breathed Milly, her horror mounting. 'Murray Eddington.'

'Cheers Mills!' Caroline beamed at her as she grabbed her notebook from her jacket pocket and scribbled it down. 'This is going to make a great front page for next week's issue!'

'You're not telling me the photographer really *did* get a shot of it happening?' said Milly faintly.

'No, sadly not,' sighed Caroline, rolling her eyes. 'Apparently, she was too busy focusing on details of the bride's dress... and the bridesmaids... and the shoes!'

'To be fair, that *is* her job,' said Milly. 'How was she to know disaster was about to strike?'

Caroline shrugged, looking mildly irritated. 'Bit of a shame, though.'

'Plenty of people had their mobiles out...' said Milly.

'You're right... maybe one of them got the money shot!'

Caroline disappeared again before Milly had the chance to say anything else. She swallowed and stared after her, not sure what to do next.

Now she knew it was Murray over there on the floor, she felt like she should go to him... but just because he'd camped out in her head for the past year and a half, it didn't mean she *knew* him. It wasn't like she could answer any questions for the paramedics when they turned up.

Milly sighed and forced herself to turn away from the scene. Her eyes came to rest on the horse, who was ambling across the overgrown lawn, the carriage leaving deep ruts in its wake. After a few lazy strides, the animal came to an abrupt stop, ducked its head and started to rip up great gobfuls of greenery.

'Can I have everyone's attention please?'

The shout came from behind her, along with the tinkling of a knife against a champagne glass. Milly whirled around only to spot a short man wearing a grey top hat standing in the doorway of the hotel. For some reason, he had a decidedly smug smile on his face.

'The bride and groom kindly request that you all make your way back inside to join them – dinner is about to be served.'

'You're kidding me?!' muttered Milly. How could they even *think* of going ahead with the reception while their best man was lying in an unconscious heap in the carpark?

It quickly became clear that she was the only one with such reservations, though. There was a sudden mass exodus towards the hotel, and Milly was jostled as guests barged past her, gossiping about what had just happened - sounding excited rather than concerned.

Feeling like a fish swimming against the tide, Milly moved further away from the hotel - crossing the car park. Everyone else might be happy to leave him to his fate now that the excitement was over, but *someone* had to make sure Murray was okay until the ambulance turned up!

'Mills, where are you going?' said Caroline, appearing in front of her.

'I just want to check on Murray…' she said quickly. 'Is he still bleeding?'

'Breathe, Milly!' ordered Caroline, looking concerned. 'I couldn't see any blood… and don't worry, the ambulance is just pulling in.'

Sure enough, it swung around the corner even as she said the words.

'But… is there someone with him?' she pressed on. That strange, dizzy sensation was washing over her again.

'Yeah, don't worry,' said Caroline. 'Ian's with him. He's the hotel's first aider. The paramedics will sort him out – he'll be okay.'

'You think?' said Milly, swaying slightly.

'I know! Come on, I'm taking you inside,' said Caroline, grabbing hold of her arm and starting to lead her back towards the door. 'You're as white as a sheet. You need a drink and something to eat. I had no idea you were such a delicate flower!'

Milly winced.

'Bad choice of words there?' said Caroline with a smirk.

Milly just shrugged and then paused again to watch as the ambulance made its way back out of the carpark. They'd certainly made short work of that! Considering there was no sign of Murray amongst the handful of people it had left in its wake, she could only guess that he was on board.

'I might just go home,' she said vaguely.

'Rubbish!' said Caroline. 'You're in no fit state to go anywhere. Besides - you can't abandon me now. You just need some bad canapes inside you, and you'll be as right as rain!'

Milly wanted to argue, but she simply didn't have the energy. She let Caroline steer her back inside the hotel. Maybe she'd be able to slip away after the meal. She definitely wasn't up for bopping around at the disco… especially considering any chance of dancing with Murray had just disappeared with the wailing of the ambulance's sirens.

One glass of fizz, a bit of food… and then she'd make her way back up the hill towards home. Perhaps she'd stop in Bendall's on her way, though. They had a special offer on ice cream at the moment – and right now, she could do with a tub or two!

## CHAPTER 6

MURRAY

Murray closed his eyes. The greenish-bluey blur of the marshes sliding past the taxi window was making him feel a bit queasy. It was Monday morning... and he still wasn't feeling quite right.

*Also - how was it Monday already?!*

He couldn't believe he'd been stuck in the hospital for the entire weekend. According to the frazzled, overworked nurses who'd been in charge of him, Murray had still been unconscious when he'd arrived in the ambulance. Even when he *did* regain his faculties, it had taken him a little while to come around properly... and even longer for him to piece together what had happened.

As soon as the strong painkillers started to work their magic – taking his headache from full-on tympani to more of an annoying background bongo - Murray had asked to go home.

*Fat chance of that, though!*

The nurse had basically laughed in his face and told him he wouldn't be going anywhere until he'd had his head scanned... and after that, he'd be sticking around for observation until he'd managed to convince the doctors he wasn't about to keel over.

When Murray asked how long it would all take – an hour? or two? - she'd laughed again. Then she'd casually tossed the words "oh, probably about a week" over her shoulder as she'd beetled off to deal with another patient - who was loudly demanding strawberry jelly at the other end of the ward.

Luckily for Murray – she'd either had a slightly evil sense of humour, or the ward had simply become too busy to waste a bed on the guy who'd got into a fight with a bunch of flowers. Either way, the scan must have come back clear - because he'd been sent packing after just two nights.

If he was honest, Murray was feeling like a bit of a fraud. There didn't seem to be much wrong with him other than the modest bump on his head where the bouquet had landed. It felt like he should have something a bit more dramatic to show for the whole thing – especially considering the chaos it had caused.

Apparently.

He couldn't remember much about it.

Stretching in his seat, Murray let out a soft groan.

There might not be much wrong with him other than the bump and a few bruises – presumably from where he'd hit the ground – but boy did he ache!

Murray's suit didn't look much happier than he did. A couple of days spent screwed up on a chair beside his hospital bed certainly hadn't been very kind to it.

He blew out a long breath, impatient to get home so that he could get changed, grab some paracetamol and then a much-needed nap. Still... he knew he should thank his lucky stars that he *was* on his way home. It could have been so much worse. At least he hadn't broken anything.

Well... maybe his pride... but that was another story!

'Heavy weekend?'

Murray's eyes met those of the taxi driver in the rear-view mirror. Brian Singer was grinning at him – clearly taking his rumpled appearance as the sign of a walk-of-shame after a damn good blow-out.

*If only!*

'Something like that!' said Murray, forcing himself to return Brian's smile, even though it seemed to offend the bongo player inside his skull - if the renewed thumping was anything to go by.

Murray had called Brian to pick him up from the train station. He hadn't really felt up to facing public transport, but the hospital was a bit too far from Crumbleton to warrant a taxi all the way back. At least the short train ride had meant he could be returning from anywhere. If the chatty cabby didn't know what had happened at the wedding, Murray certainly wasn't going to be the one to fill him in.

He knew that it wasn't really his fault he'd got walloped over the head by a flying bridal bouquet, but it was hardly something he wanted to broadcast either. If Murray had his way, the whole incident would never be mentioned again…

'Well – your weekend can't have been as bad as one of the blokes who went to the Dolphin and Anchor wedding on Saturday!' chuckled Brian.

*Huh, so much for keeping the whole thing quiet!*

'Oh?' said Murray vaguely.

'Poor blighter had quite a nasty accident!' said Brian. 'He got clonked on the head by a bunch of flowers.'

'Really?' muttered Murray, cringing slightly.

'Yep – had to be airlifted out of town too!'

Murray let out a snort of surprised laughter, but luckily Brian mistook it as a sound of shock.

'I know – I couldn't believe it either,' he said, his eyes going wide in the rear-view mirror. 'I wasn't in town at the time – I had a fare over to Crumbleton Sands – but I heard all about it when I got back. I can't imagine where the helicopter managed to land – maybe they did one of those hover-manoeuvres where they haul you up in a basket?'

'Erm… maybe?' said Murray. The pounding in his head was growing even louder – probably from the sheer pressure of trying to stop a wave of giggles from escaping.

'Anyway,' said Brian. 'I heard there were police and ambulances and the fire brigade and everything… though I'm not exactly sure what they were all doing there.'

'No… I can't imagine,' choked Murray as a full-blown chortle erupted from his throat.

Brian shot him a look of concern. Perhaps he thought he was crying or something.

'Ah now, lad!' he said consolingly. 'I'm sure whoever it was will be fine… though they *did* say there was an awful lot of blood!'

Murray bit his lip and leaned back against the seat, shaking his head in amusement. He could only marvel at Crumbleton's storytelling prowess. Of course, he *had* been unconscious for the whole thing, so there was a faint possibility there really had been a helicopter… and fire engines… and the police… but somehow, he doubted it!

As for there being blood everywhere…? If that was true, it certainly hadn't come from him. Murray didn't even have a scratch on him – just the less-than-impressive bump on his noggin.

Brian was still chattering away in the front seat about how much he wished he could have seen it all.

'Probably a good thing I missed it, though… I'm not great with blood, me!'

Murray closed his eyes and let it all wash over him. He *really* needed that paracetamol and a lie-down!

'They must have picked the bloke up nice and fast,' Brian continued, unmoved by Murray's silence. 'I was only gone for about an hour, and everything was quiet by the time I got back. Outside, at least – the disco inside was quite loud. I wanted a game of darts in the bar, but the best man pretty much growled at me, so I decided to give it a miss after all.'

*Best man?*

Murray let out another low groan. There was only one person that could have been. Josh must have been in seventh heaven when he'd been carted away in the ambulance!

'Must have been one heck of a party you've been to, if you're only just getting back now,' said Brian, giving him a sympathetic glance in the mirror. He clearly thought Murray was suffering from a hangover to end all hangovers rather than a sunflower-induced concussion.

Murray just forced a rueful smile. He wasn't about to put him right. 'Reckon you can drop me off at the wharf?'

'That's a little way out,' said Brian in surprise. 'Sure you don't want me to take you into town instead? You look like you could do with a couple of cups of Mabel's coffee and a bacon sarnie before you even think about rowing back home.'

Murray shook his head, and then promptly wished he hadn't. 'The wharf's fine, thanks.'

As much as Murray would love a coffee right now, he didn't want to reappear in town looking like the crumpled ghost of a best man doomed to wander Crumbleton in a morning suit for all eternity. Besides, he smelled like hospital – a strange mixture of stress-sweat and disinfectant. He needed a shower, a change of clothes and a lie-down.

Plus... he couldn't risk bumping into Milly in this state. He'd been so excited to see her on Saturday, but now... he wasn't so sure! He had no idea if she'd witnessed his bouquet-headbutt-of-shame, but judging by how intrigued Brian seemed to be about the whole thing, he wasn't about to kid himself. Milly would have heard all the details by now – both the real ones and the extended director's cut, complete with blooper reel!

'Nearly there,' said Brian, glancing at him again, clearly wondering if he was about to disgrace himself by puking all over the back of his pristine cab.

'Mm,' said Murray vaguely.

'You know... they never did find out what happened to the bouquet after it knocked that chap out.'

'Uh huh?' said Murray.

'Yeah... weird, huh? Someone must have taken it, I guess. Whopping great big thing it was too, apparently. It must have really done some damage. Personally, I think I would have ducked if I saw it coming straight for me!' He pulled a face and drew the taxi to a gentle halt.

Murray simply smiled and started rummaging in the pocket of his ridiculous, tailed jacket for his wallet. He couldn't wait to get out of the car - he didn't think he'd ever been so happy to see his boat waiting for him!

'Thanks for the ride – keep the change,' he said, handing over a couple of notes.

'Right you are,' said Brian, taking the money with a grateful nod. 'Now – remember what I said – bacon sarnie and a coffee and you'll be as right as rain. Reckon you won't be partying quite so hard again for a little while, eh?'

'Probably not,' said Murray with a rueful smile before making a break for it.

Crossing the road in front of the cab, Murray took a deep breath - glad of the fresh air after the stuffy hospital ward followed by the scent of Brian's air freshener. He turned and raised his hand to wave Brian off, only to catch the taxi driver eyeballing his crumpled suit with raised eyebrows.

*Uh oh!*

Murray hurriedly started to untie the boat and then hopped down. He was uncomfortably aware that Brian was watching his every move. Something told him that he'd just been rumbled.

Taking his seat, Murray grabbed his oars and began to row, keen to put as much distance between himself and the taxi as he could.

'Blasted thing!' he muttered, cursing the stupid jacket as it immediately cut into his arms.

Pausing briefly, he yanked it off, not caring in the slightest when the movement resulted in a loud ripping sound. He just tossed it onto the grubby deck and rolled his shoulders.

*There... much better.*

Grabbing the oars again, Murray pulled hard. The boat shot through the water, leaving Brian Singer staring after him.

## CHAPTER 7

MILLY

Monday mornings were usually Milly's happy place. She knew that probably made her a bit weird – but she didn't really care! There was nothing quite like the buzz of excitement she felt, opening up her shop for the first time after the weekend.

*Milly's Flowers* was her domain. She'd built it up from scratch – and it still made her heart flutter with a heady mixture of pride and excitement. The start of a new week meant fresh deliveries and the chance to try out design ideas she'd dreamed up over the weekend. At least… that's what Mondays *usually* meant.

Today though? Not so much!

This particular Monday morning found Milly dragging her feet down the narrow wooden staircase that led from her cosy flat to the door right next to her shop below. The thought of launching into the day's tasks made her feel exhausted rather than excited, and the sound of the shop phone - already demanding her attention - made her want to turn around and head straight back up to bed.

Milly paused to glance at her watch. It was still early. Whoever it was could wait. They'd call back if it was important.

*Seriously – what kind of attitude is that? Pull yourself together!*

Milly had been giving herself a good talking to inside her own head every ten minutes or so since she'd returned home on Saturday… but it was yet to have the desired effect. She was in a funk to end all funks. Despite her best efforts not to think about the "great wedding disaster" - as she'd dubbed it - her mind was still full of it… *and* Murray.

Even if she didn't count Murray's accident, it had to be the weirdest wedding she'd ever been to. The plates of food had barely touched the tables before they were snatched away again by the harassed and decidedly embarrassed-looking waiting staff. It had almost felt like there was someone out in the kitchens with a giant stopwatch, timing every bite.

That wasn't the worst bit, though. The speeches had started the minute everyone sat down to eat, and they were still going on by the time Milly made a break for it. In fact, she'd bet her shop and everything in it that the short guy with the top hat who'd stepped in for Murray was still down at the Dolphin and Anchor right now - droning on about his "special friendship" with the bride and groom.

In the end, Milly had ducked out before pudding was served. She'd felt awful about abandoning Caroline – but by that point in proceedings, her excuse hadn't even been a lie. Her headache was in full bloom, and she'd been seriously happy to get out of there.

Poor Caroline - Milly had barely given her a second to react before she'd clambered to her feet and bolted for the doors. Usually, her finely honed people-pleasing gene would have stopped her from even *thinking* about leaving in the middle of a wedding. In this case though, the happy couple had been busy shrugging into their own jackets as she legged it out of the room… so she didn't feel too bad!

After nipping into Bendall's for an essential ice cream stock-up on her way back up the hill, Milly had locked the door behind her and gone to ground for the rest of the weekend. She'd worked her way steadily through her own body weight of raspberry ripple and mint choc chip while doing her best not to think about the wedding… or the fact that the flowers she'd hand-tied had knocked the man of her dreams unconscious.

'Gah!' she groaned as she fiddled with the keys and unlocked the shop at a snail's pace.

She didn't know why she'd pinned such high hopes on seeing Murray at the wedding. Perhaps because weddings were meant to be inherently romantic. Whatever the reason, she'd somehow managed to convince herself that the weekend would deliver her very own rom-com moment.

Okay... okay... perhaps that had been asking a *bit* much.

Frankly, she'd have settled for a proper introduction, a nice conversation... and maybe a dance. Instead, the poor guy had been carted off in an ambulance before she'd even managed to say a word to him. It was hard not to take the whole thing as some huge, cosmic sign from the universe that romance simply wasn't for her.

To make matters worse, Milly had no idea if Murray was okay. She was desperate to find out – but she'd quickly realised that she had no way of actually doing so. She didn't have his mobile number... and she didn't know who his friends were... because she didn't really *know* him. Obsessing over him for a year and a half didn't count when it mattered!

So – like the grown-up she was – Milly had decided the best way to deal with the whole thing was to hide in her flat and pretend it had never happened. Unfortunately, the rude arrival of Monday morning meant *that* was no longer an option. Somehow, she had a feeling the Great Wedding Disaster was likely to be the topic on everyone's lips.

'Are you going to actually open that door or are we just going to spend the day out here?!'

Milly jumped and then glared over her shoulder at Jo. She had no idea how long her trainee had been standing there but going by the curious look on the girl's face, it had been a little while.

'Sorry,' she said, shaking her head, 'I was miles away.'

Pushing the door open, Milly made the most of the beeping burglar alarm to buy her a few seconds before she had to actually enter into any kind of conversation. She dashed over to the cubby hole to disarm it, and then took a deep breath before heading back through to the shop, plastering a smile on her face.

'Good weekend?' she said, wandering over to the till.

'Who cares about my weekend!' said Jo, shrugging out of her patchwork coat, 'I want to hear all about the wedding!'

'Oh,' said Milly, her heart sinking. She'd been expecting this, but not quite so soon! 'Well-'

*Saved by the bell!*

Milly had never been so happy to be interrupted by the phone. She made an apologetic face at Jo and practically lunged for the handset.

'Milly's Flowers – Milly speaking!' she trilled.

'Oh thank heavens, I've been calling all weekend.'

Milly raised her eyebrows in surprise. It was a gruff, male voice that she couldn't place.

'How can I help?' she said curiously.

'It's Wilfred Manning.'

'Uh huh?' said Milly, racking her brain and

wondering whether the name should mean something to her.

'We met at the wedding on Saturday – I was the bloke with the horse and cart.'

'Oh!' said Milly in surprise. 'How can I help you, Wilfred?'

'Well… it's like this…' Wilfred trailed off, sounding awkward. There was a deep sigh before he carried on. 'Were there any plants in the bride's bouquet that might be poisonous?'

'Poisonous?!' said Milly. The word escaped in a high-pitched treble. Was this about Murray?! It was bad enough that her flowers had knocked him out, but if she'd somehow managed to poison him too—

'Yes – for horses, I mean,' said Wilfred, interrupting her spiralling panic. 'Everyone's blaming Hercules for eating the flowers.'

'Hercules?' echoed Milly.

'The horse!' harrumphed Wilfred. 'Keep up!'

Milly thought back to the small, slightly rotund pony who'd barely been able to keep his eyes open. It was a pretty grand name for the little guy!

'Look,' said Wilfred. 'I don't *think* he ate it – but there was a lot going on what with that bloke on the ground and the ambulance arriving. He might have nibbled a flower or two - and I just want to check he'll be alright. He seems a bit depressed, that's all!'

'Right…' said Milly, shaking her head as she tried to get it on straight. 'So… there were cornflowers, gerberas, sunflowers, roses and gypsophila. I don't think any of them are poisonous – and I don't use sprays or anything…'

'Well – it's a start,' said Wilfred.

'I'll need to do a bit of research just to check the flowers are horse safe, though!' she added. 'Can I call you back?'

'Please!' said Wilfred. 'I've been *that* worried about the little fellow. He's my best friend. I'd never forgive myself if something happened to him.'

'Of course,' said Milly, melting slightly. 'I'll double-check now and call you straight back.'

'What on earth was all that about?' said Jo, the minute she put the phone down.

Milly sighed. The last thing she wanted to do was mention the wedding again, but there was no way around it.

'The owner of the horse from the wedding wants to know if any of the flowers are toxic for horses,' she said, firing up the shop's laptop so that she could start researching. 'Looks like Hercules helped himself to a bit of a feast!'

'Blimey,' said Jo, shaking her head. 'If you ask me, that bouquet was cursed. Killing off the best man *and* the horse? Whatever's next… the bride and groom?'

'Hush!' hissed Milly, her eyes going wide as she glanced over at the door to double-check they were still alone. The last thing she needed was any hint of supposedly cursed wedding flowers to get out. People were so weirdly suspicious around weddings as it was. 'No one's dead!'

'Yet!' said Jo, looking excited. 'I mean, no one's seen the best man since the accident, have they? He could have bled to death in the ambulance!'

Milly stared at Jo, feeling slightly sick for a second – and then common sense kicked in again. 'There wasn't any blood.'

'Oh,' said Jo, looking disappointed. 'But he *did* lose several teeth!'

'What? How do you know that?' said Milly.

'Kendra told me!' she said. 'According to her, the bloke fell flat on his face and there were teeth everywhere. Actually... I was going to ask if I could have a bit longer for lunch so that I can go down and help Kendra look for them in the gravel.'

'Eww!' said Milly. 'Why?!'

'Because it would be cool!' said Jo with a shrug. 'What do you think?'

'I think I need a coffee,' said Milly, opening the till and grabbing some money. 'Here,' she added, thrusting it in Jo's direction. 'Go find Mabel and grab us both an extra-large cappuccino – or whatever you fancy.'

Jo's eyes lit up. 'Thanks, Milly!'

'And not a word to anyone about cursed bouquets, or unconscious best men... *or* poisoned horses!' she said with a frown. 'Got it?'

'Fine!' said Jo, letting out a long sigh. 'It'd be *great* publicity, though.'

'*Not* the kind I'm looking for!' said Milly, shaking her head. 'It's bad enough Caroline's going to cover the whole thing in the paper.'

'She is?!' said Jo. 'Do you think she'll mention my name?'

'Why would she?' said Milly.

'I *did* do the flowers,' said Jo.

'You tied a couple of buttonholes!' chuckled Milly, deciding not to mention the fact that she'd had to re-do both of them because they'd come undone. Jo still had a lot to learn.

'I delivered them, though,' said Jo. 'I should at least get an honourable mention!'

'Coffee – pronto!' laughed Milly, ushering Jo towards the door.

Milly let out a sigh of relief as Jo shot her a broad smile and then disappeared. She didn't really want a coffee, but it was worth it just to buy herself a couple of minutes' peace and quiet.

She'd love nothing more than to forget all about the wedding and get on with her week - but first, she needed to check that Hercules was definitely going to be okay after his run-in with the bouquet. If only she could do the same thing when it came to Murray!

Milly frowned. Maybe she could visit him in hospital? There was just one problem with that – she didn't know which ward he was on. Would they even let her see him, anyway? Besides, he might already be home for all she knew.

*Urgh – this was going to drive her insane!*

'Caroline!' breathed Milly. She'd call Caroline. If anyone knew what was going on, it'd be her friend. If she was careful, she could make it sound like she was just calling about the newspaper article…

## CHAPTER 8

MURRAY

It ended up being a bit of a tricky trip back home across the salt marshes, and Murray didn't think he'd ever been so grateful to reach the old trawler.

The flooding from the heavy rains they'd endured for weeks on end had finally started to recede, and the water levels had dropped significantly since Saturday. It meant he'd had to stick to the deeper channels, steering the boat carefully to prevent himself from getting stuck.

If he was being honest, it would probably have been easier to walk home – taking to the narrow, hidden pathways that criss-crossed the wetland. You had to know the marshes like the back of your hand to be able to follow them without taking a wrong turn and ending up knee-deep in the brackish, muddy water. As Marsh Ranger, he knew the paths better than anyone -

but frankly, he didn't have the energy for a long walk. Rowing home had been hard enough.

The minute he climbed on board, leaving the boat tied up below, Murray started to unbutton his shirt. He couldn't wait to jump in the shower.

Letting himself inside, Murray blew out a long sigh of relief. He couldn't wait to wash the lingering scent of the hospital out of his hair. Then he'd climb back into his usual uniform of tatty shorts and a soft, slouchy tee shirt. He'd had enough suit-wearing to last him a lifetime.

Peering around his home, Murray felt the tension start to drain from his shoulders, and his headache eased off a couple of notches. The place always had this effect on him – it was why he loved living out here so much. The trawler might look a bit rough from the outside, but inside it was a cosy oasis - complimented by all the mod cons. The waterfall shower he'd installed was at the top of his list of favourites right now – closely followed by the coffee machine.

By this point, he'd stripped right down to his boxers. He was so intent on heading straight for the bathroom for the longest soak of his life that he'd dropped a trail of clothing behind him – he'd pick it up later! He was just about to grab a towel from the cupboard when his Sat Phone caught his eye.

'Damn!' he muttered, glowering at the flashing red light that signalled a bunch of new messages.

For a second, Murray contemplated ignoring them

until he'd had the chance to shower. After all, no one knew he was home – so it wasn't like there was any rush.

But… what if they were important?

It wasn't in his nature to ignore a job once he knew it needed his attention. The thought of that little red light demanding his attention the minute he finished would just ruin his longed-for shower.

Murray strode over to the desk and punched the button – keen to get it over with.

*'Murray mate, it's Philip!'* The bridegroom's voice boomed around the cabin.

*'And Elizabeth!'* came the bride's slightly muffled whine in the background.

*'Yeah... and the wife! Anyway, we're at the airport. Just wanted to leave you a message before we catch our flight. We wanted to say - don't worry – you didn't ruin anything.'*

*'Well, he did a little bit,'* huffed Elizabeth.

*'Okay,'* agreed Philip. *'She's right, you did ruin things a little bit. Everything ran late for a while – after waiting for the ambulance and all that – but we made up most of the time by cutting each course of the meal down to seven minutes. That fixed it...'*

*'Only because we missed dessert!'* hissed Elizabeth.

*'Yeah. That. Anyway, we had a brilliant time...'*

*'Apart from Josh's speech – tell him, Philip!'*

*'Apart from Josh's speech!'* Philip agreed. *'It went on forever. We had to call our own toast to shut him up in the*

*end, but he just carried on again afterwards and he was still going when we left!'*

'That's our flight!' Elizabeth squealed. *'Our flight just got called. Hang up already!'*

*'Catch you when we get back.'*

*'Give me the phone!'*

*'Don't snatch, woman!'*

That was the end of the message. Murray let out a long sigh.

'No, no,' he said to thin air. 'I'm fine… don't worry about me… in fact - don't even ask how my head is!'

The phone beeped as it clicked through to the next message.

*'Dude, it's Josh.'*

'Ah maaan!' sighed Murray, rubbing his forehead and closing his eyes as he wondered what he'd done in a previous life to deserve this.

*'Way to go for looking like a total knob by headbutting a bunch of flowers!'* Josh's voice was full of laughter. *'Seriously though, mate – I'm sorry that happened to you.'*

He didn't sound very sorry. In fact, he sounded… gleeful.

*'Anyway, just wanted to tell you not to worry – I jumped in and saved the day. Good thing I had a speech prepared, eh?'*

Murray tutted and rolled his eyes before thinking better of it – it made everything hurt.

*'Everyone loved it. I guess it was more meaningful and heartfelt coming from me anyway… you know… considering*

*I actually know Philip! Plus... you know... I didn't embarrass them by getting knocked on my butt by a bunch of flowers. By the way - you nearly ruined their honeymoon by making them late for their flight!'*

Murray let out a low growl.

*'A-ny-way,'* Josh's voice continued in a self-congratulatory singsong, *'would you like to hear my speech – just so you're in the loop?'*

'No!' Murray yelled at the machine, but it clearly didn't hear him because Josh's voice turned into a strange kind of monotone as he started to read.

*'My lords, ladies and gentlemen – welcome to best man two-point-oh...'*

'Seriously?!' huffed Murray. One thing was for sure, he wasn't about to stand there and listen to the idiot waffle on for an age. He quickly skipped to the next message.

*'Hi! I hope this is the right number for Murray Eddington, best man from the Williams wedding at the Dolphin and Anchor on Saturday?'*

'I wish it wasn't!' murmured Murray.

*'This is Caroline Cook, editor of the Crumbleton Times and Echo. I'd love to get an interview with you about what happened. I hope you're feeling better. I'm going to be running a feature on the incident this week. Front page. I'm still trying to track down a picture, but a few words from you would be great. I'm hoping Milly Rowlands from the flower shop will give me a quote about the flowers – maybe something about how often people get into life-threatening*

*fisticuffs with bridal bouquets... add a bit of humour to the tragedy of the accident, you know? Anyway, call me!'*

'No chance,' said Murray, listening as Caroline reeled off her phone number before hanging up.

Thankfully, that was the end of the messages, and Murray hit the "delete all" button with an added flourish of his middle finger when the machine asked him if he'd like to listen to them again.

So much for anyone caring if he was actually okay. Sure, he *was* a bit embarrassed about the whole thing, but he could have been seriously hurt for all any of them knew... not that any of them had bothered to ask.

He huffed, this time at himself for being such a needy wet blanket. Plus, he wasn't being fair – at least Caroline Cook had said she hoped that he was okay! Plus... she'd mentioned Milly. Not that he was going to think about that right now.

Heading over to the cupboard, Murray started to rummage around for a big, fluffy bath towel – doing his best to pretend Milly's name wasn't still ringing in his ears. He'd had such high hopes for the weekend. He didn't really know why he'd thought it would finally be his chance to meet her properly... and maybe even do something about his ridiculous mega-crush.

Somehow, Murray got the feeling he was going to remember this wedding forever – but not for the reason he'd been hoping. He hadn't even had the chance to speak to Milly before being carted off in an ambulance. She was the only reason he'd agreed to be a part of the whole thing in the first place, and he'd blown it. Maybe it just wasn't meant to be. Maybe the kiss they'd shared was it for them – the sum total of their connection.

Murray's shoulders slumped, and his headache ramped up again – thrumming against his skull with renewed vigour.

Maybe it was all for the best. What did he have to offer someone like Milly anyway? He lived in an abandoned boat, for goodness' sake! She wouldn't be interested in an idiot like him!

Slinging the towel over his shoulder, Murray headed for the shower, feeling decidedly depressed.

## CHAPTER 9

### MILLY

Maybe borrowing the council's knackered old rowing boat wasn't the best idea she'd ever had. It was always tied up at the wharf, available for anyone to use in case of emergency (usually involving stranded sheep or drunken shenanigans). It was mainly used by birdwatchers these days, but if the layer of weeds growing inside it was anything to go by, it hadn't been taken out for a while.

Milly let out a low stream of swear words as the boat scooted around in the muddy water, arcing in a stubborn circle as it refused to obey her commands.

'Forwards, you stupid thing,' she growled. 'Preferably in a straight line!'

Okay, so maybe her plan had a few flaws. She'd never been particularly good at rowing, but as far as she knew, there wasn't another way to get to Murray's trawler. Why he couldn't live on dry land like everyone else was beyond her. What was wrong with a nice, normal house anyway?

'Will… you… just… behave?!' she grunted, yanking on the oars and then almost dropping one as the boat wobbled precariously.

Milly really needed to get this situation under control before it ended in disaster. After all, she'd been brought up in Crumbleton, so it wasn't as though she'd never been out on a boat before. She'd paddled around the marshes plenty of times as a kid. It had just been… a while!

'Okay, okay, that's more like it!' she cheered as she found a slightly deeper channel of water, and the boat began to glide forward. Now all she had to do was stay calm until she got there.

Calm. Right. Because that was easy to achieve when she was about to turn up at Murray's home – uninvited - after a bouquet she'd created had landed him in hospital. Oh, and not to forget - the pair of them didn't actually know each other. In fact, there was a good chance he might not even recognise her.

'Breathe!' Milly hissed at herself.

Maybe it was time to search for a few positives in this hair-brained plan of hers – just to give herself something to cling to as she rowed.

Positive number one – according to Caroline, Murray was out of hospital. Unfortunately, this titbit had come at a high price. Milly's clumsy attempts at extracting information had been no match for

Caroline's finely tuned Spidey-senses. In the end, she'd been forced to own up to her long-held crush... *and* the kiss that had started the whole thing before Caroline would agree to help her.

Still, it had worked a treat. After going all soppy for a few seconds, her friend had called the ward and pretended to be Murray's sister, before reporting straight back to Milly. By the sound of things, he should already be home.

Positive number two – she was being proactive! After eighteen months of wishing and dreaming and sighing and hoping that something might happen with Murray, Milly was finally on her way to talk to him. Sure... it was so that she could apologise for playing a part in a possible concussion... but it was a starting point, right?

Milly had left Jo in charge of the shop, with detailed instructions on how to lock up if she wasn't back in time. She'd then dashed in and out of the shops on her way down the hill, filling a bag with basic groceries – including cake. Cake always made things better!

Positive number three? At least there wasn't anyone around to witness what a prat she was making out of herself in this stupid boat!

Blowing out an exhausted breath, Milly pulled on the oars again. This was much harder than she remembered. She *had* hoped it would all come back to her – like riding a bike or something... but at this rate, she'd arrive at Murray's place in a hot, sweaty state of disrepair.

*If* she could find his place!

This was another thing she hadn't thought through properly. Even though she had a rough idea where the trawler was, the marshes were always changing… and they were vast! Plus, everything looked very different from her perch at water level. It was a *lot* harder to see where she was going with all the stupid bloody rushes and tufts of grass blocking the view.

It was *fine*. Of *course* she'd find it!

Milly wasn't in any kind of rush. She'd already called Wilfred back to confirm that Hercules was going to be fine and dandy after his elicit snack at the wedding, and she'd left Jo in charge of the shop.

'ARGH!' Milly squealed as a startled heron took flight from a clump of reeds right next to her. She jumped so badly that the entire boat rocked like a bucking bronco.

'Calm! Breathe!' she muttered again, sounding like a very shrill stuck record.

*It was just a heron. Nothing to worry about!*

No… if she really wanted something to worry about, it was being lost out here on the marshes all night. What if she couldn't find the trawler? What if she *did* find it, and Murray wasn't there? He could be out counting frogs, or something equally as bizarre for all she knew. He *was* the Marsh Ranger, after all. He could be anywhere.

But then… considering he'd just been released from hospital, surely he'd be taking it easy?

Well… there wasn't any point going around in circles inside her own head, was there? Not when she was having enough trouble stopping the boat from doing just that.

Milly frowned around her, trying to see through the thick reeds and rushes, desperate for a glimpse of some kind of landmark that might help her get her bearings again.

'Admit it, you're lost!' she huffed.

What on earth had she been thinking, coming out here on a mission to apologise for something that wasn't even her fault to start with? It was probably the worst excuse in the history of excuses for turning up at someone's home unannounced. If anyone was to blame for Murray's accident – it was Elizabeth. She'd been the one to choose such a ridiculously big bunch of flowers to start with.

Milly had to face facts. The only reason she was paddling around, lost in the middle of Crumbleton marshes right now was the fact that she'd finally had enough of waiting.

She wanted to meet Murray.

She wanted to see with her own eyes that he still had all his teeth - and really *was* going to be okay.

Then… she wanted to grab him and kiss his face off. After that, maybe she'd ask him on a date.

'Or maybe you could just turn around and go

home,' she whispered, her oars going still as the stupidity of her weird little mission clonked her over the head. Pausing for a beat or two, she let the boat drift idly as a curious sparrow peered at her from a nearby rush.

'What do you think I should do?' she said.

The sparrow cocked its head one way, and then the other - not taking his eyes off her. He looked like he was thinking hard.

'Don't rush,' she laughed, 'take your time!'

The sparrow let out two short peeps, bobbed its tiny body, and then flew off in a scurry of silky feathers.

'Yeah – that's what I think too,' said Milly. 'It's too late to bow out now!'

She grabbed the oars again and started to row with a newfound determination. It worked a treat for about thirty seconds.

A strange, sludgy, sliding sound came from the bottom of the boat.

'What noooooow?' Milly whined, even though it was pretty obvious *what now*. The water was getting too shallow for the boat. She could feel it dragging along the mud beneath her. That wasn't good. If she didn't watch out, she was going to get stranded… then what would she do?!

'Okay – it's fine,' she muttered, as the boat came to a dead stop. 'Don't panic, I'll just…'

She tried rowing backwards, then forwards… and then…

'Gah!' She was officially stuck.

After a couple of seconds of pure, silent horror, Milly clambered carefully to her feet. Placing one oar into the bottom of the boat, she carried the other one to the back, intent on using it as a punt. What could be more romantic than turning up, gondola-style?

Milly thrust the end of the oar into the deep mud and pushed. The boat didn't budge – but helpfully, the oar sank by about a foot.

'Not the plan!' she sighed, yanking on it to no avail. Great – now the oar was stuck too.

It took several hard tugs before the mud relinquished the paddle with a gruesome, slurping sound. Not one to give up easily, Milly chose a new spot before thrusting the oar back down into the ooze and shoving hard. This time the boat did move forward by a couple of feet… but the oar didn't come with her.

Wobbling precariously, Milly had to let go – it was either that or end up plunging backwards off the boat.

'Now what!' she gasped, staring at the oar standing straight up out of the mud like a totem pole - just out of her reach. As she watched, it started to keel over in slow-motion, before plopping backwards into the muddy water.

'Great,' she said. The word came out on a bubble of hysterical laughter, and she raised her hands to her head, winding her fingers into her hair as she stared around.

*Now what was she going to do?!*

As if by magic, the outline of the trawler materialised a little way ahead of her. She was almost there! So close... and yet so far.

The boat was stuck, she'd lost an oar, and she didn't even have Murray's phone number so that she could call him and beg for a rescue. Not that she would even if she could. The poor guy had a head injury, for goodness sake!

'Right... right... only one thing for it!' she muttered.

There was no alternative. She was going to have to roll up her jeans, take off her shoes and socks, and wade the last few hundred yards. It wasn't ideal... but then neither was knocking the object of your affection out cold with a bunch of flowers.

Getting over the edge of the boat without the whole thing capsizing turned out to be a lot harder than Milly had been expecting. For an excruciating moment, she found herself folded over the edge, clinging on for dear life with her elbows while holding on tight to her shoes, socks and shopping bag as her toes dipped into the ooze.

'Eew!' she squealed.

The bottom was even less solid than she'd been expecting... but at least the water wasn't too cold.

Straightening up, Milly had to lift one foot high before plunging it back down into the mud to take a step. This was going to take a while... but at least she knew which direction she was heading in – even if she couldn't see the trawler now that she was out of the boat. She might be close, but the reeds surrounding her made an impenetrable curtain.

The next few steps weren't too bad. She was making progress even if she looked a bit like a boozed-up tightrope walker - with her hands held high, making sure her shopping bag didn't take a dip.

Then things got seriously squidgy. Two more steps found Milly sinking up to her knees. It quickly became clear that she hadn't rolled her jeans up anywhere near far enough, and the smelly, muddy water started to soak into the denim, creeping up her thighs with remarkable speed.

Milly went to take another step forward, wrinkling her nose – only to realise that she was stuck fast. Actually – scratch that... she wasn't *just* stuck, she was sinking.

*Oops!*

Wriggling around, trying to get one leg unstuck, she wobbled precariously. Okay, that wasn't good – she could do without faceplanting right into the mess.

'Murray Eddington, it's lucky you're cute!' she grumbled. 'Now what am I going to do?!'

## CHAPTER 10

MURRAY

The hot water cascading over his shoulders felt blissful. Murray had already been in the shower for what felt like an age. He really should get out... but frankly, after more than two days spent in the same clothes, he was going to make the most of feeling clean again.

Ten more minutes, then he'd re-trace his steps and grab the trail of clothes he'd left strewn across the trawler and dump them into his laundry basket. If he had the energy.

Scrunching his eyes closed, Murray turned his face upwards and let the water trickle through his hair. He'd already washed it, carefully avoiding the bump as he'd gingerly massaged his scalp. It was still decidedly tender to the touch, and even the gentle patter of the water was almost too much to bear. He probably should have left it for a day or two, but frankly, the eau-de-hospital had to go.

Okay… that was as much as his head could take! Murray turned again – and then paused. He opened his eyes, going completely still for a second. He could swear he'd just heard something…

It almost sounded like someone calling his name… but that was impossible. He had to be hearing things – which wasn't a good sign! There was no other explanation for it, though.

There was never anyone around out here in the middle of the marshes - that was the joy of the place. The trawler was a good distance from the town itself, and it was *very* rare sounds travelled that far – and then only when the wind was coming from that direction and there was a particularly rowdy party going on in the Dolphin and Anchor.

'Probably just a bird,' he muttered.

Shrugging, Murray leaned one hand against the wall. It was getting pretty steamy in there now – almost time to call it a day. He'd get dry, gather his clothes and then maybe treat himself to a nap before indulging in a coffee, and then…

*Wait – there it was again!*

Murray quickly turned the water off, cocking his head to one side, barely daring to breathe.

'Help! Murray? You there? Heeeelp!'

Okay – that *definitely* wasn't inside his head.

Clambering out of the shower, Murray quickly

grabbed his towel and wrapped it around his waist. He hurried out into his bedroom and then paused for a brief second.

*Should he grab some clothes?*

*No.*

Whoever it was out there calling for him had sounded more than a little bit desperate. Dashing through the living room, he headed straight for the door and burst out onto the deck – and spotted the problem immediately.

The sight in front of him brought him to an abrupt halt.

It was Milly. She was up to her knees in mud… and it was pretty clear she couldn't move an inch.

He sucked in a breath, wondering if he was hallucinating. For the life of him, he couldn't think what she'd be doing all the way out there in the middle of the marshes!

'Hi?' she said.

The single, uncertain word made him snap back to reality. She needed his help. Best he got her out of the mud now and asked questions later.

Glancing down at his towel, he let out a sigh. This *wasn't* quite the way he'd pictured their first official meeting… then again, neither was getting knocked out by a bunch of flowers, and there was a good chance she'd witnessed that. It looked like they were destined to keep meeting when the embarrassment-factor was dialled up to the maximum setting.

As much as he'd *really* like to go and put some clothes on, he could hardly ask her to hang tight until he'd got changed, could he? After all, this was an emergency!

Okay, maybe *not* an emergency in the usual sense of the word. There weren't crocodiles out there or anything like that... and it looked like she'd already sunk about as far as she was going to go. Even so, it didn't seem fair to disappear again.

'Erm... Murray?' This time her voice had a definite edge of concern to it, and he realised he hadn't said anything to her yet. He was just standing there, staring at her.

'Milly?' he called.

'Yeah,' she shouted back, sounding both relieved, resigned and a bit sheepish. She added in a slight shrug which he found ridiculously endearing. 'Caught you at a bad time?' she added.

'You'll just have to put up with being rescued by someone wearing a towel,' said Murray, returning her shrug with one of his own.

He might have been wrong, but he could swear she'd just let out a funny little squeak. She was probably just desperate to get out of the chilly mud and back onto dry land.

'Erm... okay... let's think,' said Murray, staring around him for a moment, doing his best to ignore his throbbing head. 'I know – let's start with you throwing

## FLOWERS GO FLYING IN CRUMBLETON

me your shoes and socks. You're going to need your hands free for the rescue mission.'

'Okay...' said Milly, sounding a bit unsure. 'Here - catch!'

The balled-up socks came hurtling towards him, and Murray caught them easily before tossing them onto the deck of the trawler. He managed to snatch the first trainer out of mid-air with no problem, but then Milly threw the second one a bit too hard. It came hurtling towards him, and he just managed to duck in time to avoid a second bump on the head.

'Sorry!' she gasped as the trainer bounced harmlessly onto the deck just behind him. 'Your poor head!'

'It's fine – you missed!' he chuckled. He'd been far too caught up with making sure that his towel stayed put to worry about the flying trainer too much.

'What about my bag?' she said.

'I'll grab it from you in a sec,' he said. 'Be right back!'

Murray turned and quickly fetched two wide, wooden planks he used when he needed to work on the hull. Then, with some careful manoeuvring, he placed them on top of the mud – creating a pathway between the trawler and Milly.

The planks were wide enough to spread Murray's weight so that he wouldn't sink – and they were just about long enough that he should be able to grab her hands.

'You're not seriously coming out here in a towel?' said Milly.

Murray raised an eyebrow, doing his best not to laugh at the little splatters of mud that now adorned her cheeks. *No one* should look this cute while stuck up to their knees in marsh water.

'Well,' he said, 'I *could* leave you out here while I go pull some clothes on. I mean, I don't want to offend you or anything!'

'I'm not offended,' she said quickly.

He might be imagining things right now, but was that a little gleam in her eyes?

Murray shook his head and then added a little shiver for good measure. He was starting to get cold. That shiver had *nothing* to do with Milly's eyes on him.

'Want me to get changed?' he said again, this time more seriously.

'No!' said Milly. 'I want to get out of here!'

'Alrighty then!' he said, breaking out his best Jim Carey impression... and then promptly wanting to face-palm. Now was definitely *not* the time to let his own special brand of craziness out to play. Then again, he could always blame it on the head injury if he had to.

*Maybe she hadn't noticed...*

Murray glanced at Milly, crossing his fingers behind his back. Unfortunately, judging by the fact that her eyebrows were now hovering somewhere near her hairline as she stared at him – he was doomed. He couldn't quite tell if it was a look of surprise, horror or amusement… and he wasn't entirely sure he wanted to find out.

'Let's get this over with,' he muttered, clambering gingerly onto the planks so that he could edge his way towards her.

## CHAPTER 11

MILLY

Murray clearly knew what he was doing, even if he *had* just broken out a scarily accurate Jim Carey impression. Milly had to hand it to him, he had pretty good balance considering he was only wearing a towel!

Milly watched him as he edged along the wide, wooden planks. The mud beneath him kept making uncouth, farty sounds and she was finding it increasingly difficult to keep a straight face.

As he drew nearer, Milly spotted one *minor* issue with his cunning plan – by the time Murray reached the end of the makeshift bridge, Milly would be eye to… well… *not quite eye* with him. To put it plainly, she was about to find herself face-to-face with the towel-covered portion of Murray Eddington.

The heat of early-onset-embarrassment stained Milly's cheeks, and the temptation to scrunch her eyes closed and pretend this wasn't happening was almost unbearable. She could hardly change her mind and send him back for some clothes at this point, could she?! Anyway, ignoring the embarrassment-factor, it wouldn't be the end of the world if the towel just happened to slip…

'Milly – are you okay?' Murray sounded worried… almost as if he'd been reading her thoughts. She *really* hoped that wasn't another one of his hidden talents - along with celebrity impressions - otherwise she was in serious trouble.

'What?' she spluttered. 'Why?' Her discomfort somehow made her sink an extra couple of inches into the mud.

'You've gone all red!' he said, looking concerned. 'Are you okay?'

'Fine, fine… I'm fine,' she blustered. 'Just… well… sinking… and keen to get out of here…'

*… preferably before she died of embarrassment!*

Milly had been taking quite a bit of comfort in the knowledge that things between them couldn't get any weirder - not after their bizarre first kiss in the carpark, followed by the weekend's Great Wedding Disaster. But this? This trumped everything!

'Here,' he said, holding out a hand for her bag. Milly passed it over and he placed it on the far side of the planks. Then, shuffling his feet and bracing himself, he held out his hands out towards her.

Milly shot one last glance at his low-slung towel before fixing her eyes on his face.

'Take my hands!' he said

Milly did as she was told, doing her best to ignore the fact that every little hair on her body stood on end at the contact.

'Ready?' he said.

'Not really,' she muttered.

Murray tugged on her hands, but Milly didn't budge. The angle was all wrong - and it just felt like she was going to yank him down on top of her if she wasn't careful. She wobbled precariously and quickly let go of him, thrusting her hands into the mud to stop herself from toppling backwards.

'Urgh!' she muttered, flicking ooze from her fingers as she straightened back up.

'Maybe grab the planks instead?' said Murray, running his fingers distractedly through his damp hair before wincing.

'You okay?' she said.

Murray grunted and gave her the tiniest nod. He was clearly in pain. The poor guy would probably be a lot *more* okay if she hadn't turned up out of the blue and forced him to stand around outside wearing nothing more than a towel while she played stuck-in-the-mud.

She needed to get out of there so that he could rest!

Milly quickly reached out and rested her palms on the rough wooden planks. If she could just shift her weight enough, she might be able to wiggle one foot free.

It probably wasn't the best look as she belly-flopped forward onto the planks... but it seemed to be working. Slowly but surely – accompanied by a horrifyingly loud farting noise - the mud relinquished its grip on one leg and then the other.

'Yes!' she crowed in triumph.

'Grab on!' said Murray.

Milly did as she was told. Taking hold of Murray's ankles, she wriggled and shuffled her way further onto the planks.

*This definitely wasn't the way she'd dreamed of feeling him up for the first time!*

Now all she had to do was get to her feet without toppling straight back in again. Easier said than done.

Milly was about to bite the bullet and use Murray's hairy legs as a human climbing frame when his hand appeared in front of her. She hesitated. By this point, she was covered in mud, and her hands were slick with the stuff. She'd already covered his ankles in gloop...

'Take my hand!' said Murray.

Milly sighed. Well... it couldn't get much worse, could it? What was a bit more mud?!

'Got ya!' Murray cheered as he hauled her to her feet with surprising strength for someone who'd been in hospital all weekend.

'Thanks!' she gasped, finding herself eye-to-eye with him. 'Erm... I'm sorry about all the mud!'

'Don't worry about it,' he said, wiping his hand on the towel and giving her a knee-meltingly slow smile. 'I'll just have to get back in the shower again. I'm not complaining.'

A strangely strangled squeak came from somewhere, and it took Milly a couple of seconds to realise it had come from her own mouth.

'Come on,' said Murray, looking concerned again. 'I think you'd better come inside and get cleaned up.'

Milly nodded. Right now, she was just grateful that he wasn't demanding answers as to why she'd been loitering - knee-deep in mud outside his home.

Murray turned and grabbed her bag in his free hand. Then, without letting go of her hand, he led the way slowly along the planks. Milly wasn't about to complain. The man of her dreams was right in front of her – practically naked - and looking decidedly edible. If it wasn't for the fact that she was covered from head to toe in splatters of stinky mud, she might have thought she'd died and gone to heaven.

Milly took a deep breath, doing her best to quell the tingles that were busy running down her arm and spreading throughout her body. It didn't help. She caught a waft of something deliciously citrussy… orange shower gel maybe?

Now she was shivering… but it had nothing to do with being cold and *everything* to do with the bare, muscled back in front of her, and the warm point of connection between her fingers and Murray's.

As soon as they reached the deck, Murray dropped her hand and turned to face her. Milly met his eyes, suddenly feeling shy.

*He looked... angry? In pain? Just plain confused?*

She wasn't sure which, but there was definitely something intense about his gaze and she had to look away after a couple of seconds.

Clearing her throat awkwardly, Milly glanced around, searching for something to say. She'd never visited the old trawler before. It was rusty and weatherworn, and she couldn't quite believe anyone would *choose* to live all the way out here on such a wreck.

'I think you'd better come in,' said Murray, beating her to it. 'You're shivering!'

'But I'm covered in mud!' said Milly, turning back to him, still feeling slightly dazed. As keen as she was to take a peek inside, the last thing she wanted to do was leave sludgy footprints in her wake.

'Hold that thought,' he said, disappearing inside the trawler.

Milly shivered again and wrapped her arms around herself.

'Here!' said Murray, reappearing in a matter of seconds and tossing something at her.

Catching the damp towel on instinct, Milly widened her eyes as she realised it was the same one he'd been wearing. She glanced at him under her

## FLOWERS GO FLYING IN CRUMBLETON

lashes. Sure enough, he'd pulled on a pair of shorts but was still deliciously shirtless.

Milly swallowed and eyeballed the towel in her hands. It was still slightly warm.

'It's already muddy,' said Murray with a shrug. 'Use it to mop your feet off a bit... then you can climb into my shower!'

'Oh... I... okay...' said Milly. The shivery feeling was now making her knees knock.

*Sit down before you fall down, Mills!*

Sinking onto the deck, Milly started to wipe as much sludge from between her toes as she could.

'Okay,' she said as soon as she was happy she wasn't about to make a mess of his home on top of everything else. 'I think I'm good.'

Murray held out a hand, and after the briefest pause, Milly took it and let him haul her back to her feet.

'Come on in!' he said, shooting a smile over his shoulder as he led her inside.

'Wow!'

Milly came to a standstill just two steps inside the door.

'You okay?' said Murray, turning to face her.

'Good, I'm good!' squeaked Milly, staring around. She felt like he'd just led her through a wormhole. How could *this* be the rusty, tatty old trawler that had been stranded in the middle of Crumbleton marshes for years? This place was... stunning!

They were standing in a living room that seemed to glow with a honey-coloured warmth. The furniture was all beautifully crafted from sanded and polished driftwood, lending a natural, beachy vibe to the room.

'You've got a wood burner?!' she gasped, spotting a lovely old, enamelled fire at the far end of the room. Okay... now she was a definitely a little bit jealous!

'My little bit of therapy,' said Murray with a smile.

Milly nodded, her eyes still darting around trying to take everything in. There were fishing floats and shells and interesting stones all over the place. She'd somehow expected it to be dark, cramped and cold in here. Instead, it was light, bright and colourful.

'Shower's through there,' said Murray, pointing towards a door at the far side of the room. 'One sec...' He rummaged in a cupboard and then handed her a huge, fluffy bath towel.

'Thanks,' she muttered, feeling awkward again.

'Use anything you want and take as long as you need... I'll make some coffee.'

'Okay... thanks,' she said again, sounding like a stuck record.

She knew she should explain herself. She needed to apologise – for the flowers... for being an idiot... for all the mud... but she wasn't keen to start while she still smelled like a bog-monster.

'Won't be long,' she mumbled. Cuddling the towel tightly to her chest, she legged it from the living room.

The door Murray had pointed her through actually

led into his bedroom – and it was just as lovely as the living room. A massive, king-sized bed sat right in the middle of the space, illuminated by perfect beams of sunlight that streamed through a row of round portholes in the hull.

The head of the bed had been crafted into bookshelves, and Milly itched to check out the titles… but there was no way she wanted to get caught snooping around his private space!

Ducking her head, she hurried across the room and pushed open another door. Sure enough, this time she found herself in the bathroom… and it was gorgeous.

There wasn't room for a bath, but the shower was huge and boasted a fancy head that promised a rainfall experience worthy of a spa. That wasn't what made her jaw drop, though. The walls were tiled with thousands of pieces of perfectly smoothed sea glass. Acres of the stuff twinkled back at her, studded with lights that made the greens, ambers and blues glow.

Turning to close the door behind her, Milly quietly locked it and hung her towel on the back. Everything was a bit damp and misty, and there was already a bath mat spread out on the floor. Her calls for help must have literally dragged Murray out of the shower.

A little shard of guilt hit Milly in the chest. Not only had she invited herself over to his place on some kind of weird fool's errand, but she'd managed to cause maximum carnage while she was at it.

Blowing out a sigh, Milly quickly stripped out of

her muddy clothes and dropped them into a heap on the floor. She'd deal with that particular problem after a wash!

Reaching into the shower, she turned the taps and tentatively held one hand under the stream. For some reason, she'd half expected the water to be stone cold – but it was perfect. Stepping under the torrent, Milly closed her eyes and did her best not to think about Murray standing naked exactly where she was just a few minutes ago.

*What was wrong with her?!*

Shaking her head, Milly opened her eyes. As much as she was tempted to stand under this delicious waterfall and soak for hours, she needed to keep her head on straight.

*Wash. Dry. Get out!*

She didn't dare outstay her welcome – not when poor Murray needed another shower thanks to her!

Quickly nicking a bit of his shower gel, Milly started to scrub at the muddy tide lines on her legs and the splatters on her arms and face.

Five minutes later, she climbed out of the shower - pink in the face and feeling so much better. She grabbed the towel and, after quickly rubbing herself dry and squeezing as much water out of her hair as possible, she wrapped it around herself like a toga.

'Okay… clothes.' She gingerly picked her jeans up with her fingertips and then screwed her nose up in disgust. There was no *way* she was going to put those back on - they stank!

Milly glanced at her jumper. It was big and baggy, she *might* just about be able to get away with it as a sweater dress… a very *very* short sweater dress. It was speckled with mud too, but it wasn't anywhere near as bad as her jeans.

A light tap on the other side of the door made Milly jump.

'Nearly done!' she squeaked.

'Cool,' said Murray, his voice slightly muffled. 'No rush. I've got some spare clothes out here for you if you want them – just a pair of shorts and a tee shirt. I'll leave them on the floor by the door. Coffee's ready when you are.'

'Oh,' said Milly, 'thanks!'

There was no reply. Did that mean he'd gone back through to the kitchen? Milly pressed her ear against the wood, listening hard. It certainly sounded like the coast was clear. Turning the lock, she opened the door a crack – just wide enough to grab the neatly folded pile of clothes before closing it again.

Milly dressed quickly and then, running her fingers through her damp hair, she wiped the steam from the mirror and checked her face.

'Nice!' she laughed, swiping her fingers across the mascara smudges beneath her eyes until she looked a tiny bit less like a panda.

*There… that would have to do.*

Milly hung her towel on the back of the door and then padded back through Murray's bedroom. She found Murray sitting at the kitchen table with a steaming cup of coffee in front of him. It took her a moment to get over the disappointment of finding him actually wearing a tee shirt.

Right… it was time to explain why she was there, ruining his Monday afternoon. She opened her mouth, but her words disappeared as Murray turned to her and grinned.

'Coffee?'

'Please!' she squeaked.

CHAPTER 12

MURRAY

Murray took a bit longer than was strictly necessary at the coffee machine. He faffed around loading the puck and tamping it down carefully. Anything to buy himself a bit of time before he had to turn around and face her again.

He was feeling… flustered. It wasn't a word he'd ever used to describe himself before, but right now, it seemed pretty fitting.

Milly looked far too adorable in his shorts and tee shirt. No one should look that beautiful wearing borrowed gear and sporting tangled, towel-dried hair. The sight of her was making him weak at the knees. Or at least – he *thought* it was Milly making him feel like that. It might be the head injury, of course!

Frankly, finding the woman of his dreams stuck in

the mud right outside his home had been the medicine he didn't know he needed. Murray had barely given his aches and pains a second thought since he'd ushered her inside the trawler... other than to register the nervous, swooping sensations in his stomach.

'Frothy milk?' he said over his shoulder, not turning to actually meet her eye in case he lost control of himself completely and did something idiotic – like pledging his undying love.

'Oooh yes please!' she said.

Huh – so it wasn't just the sight of her that made him feel all... *flippy*. The sound of her voice was enough to make him feel like he had an entire rainforest of butterflies having a party in his stomach too.

Murray swallowed and then turned back to the machine, sending super-heated steam bubbling into the milk with a strangled hiss.

*He knew just how that felt!*

At least the noise gave him an excuse not to speak for a few seconds. He was having a hard time trying to figure out how to make small-talk with the goddess sitting right behind him. He just needed a couple of seconds to pull himself together.

'Sugar?' he said when the milk was so frothy it was threatening to climb right out of the jug.

'No thanks.'

*Damnit. He was out of excuses not to turn around and face her!*

Filling the mug to the brim with the creamy concoction, Murray picked it up and turned slowly on the spot - only to find himself pinned by her eyes. Milly didn't look any more comfortable than he felt.

*Come on man – you're the host here – say something to make her relax!*

'Here,' he said, popping the coffee down in front of her and then fidgeting from foot to foot.

*Great. Nice job!*

Murray winced. Had he always been such a sarcastic asshat inside his own head? He desperately wanted to sit down. The room was suddenly a bit swimmy.

'Thanks,' said Milly, not taking her eyes off him. 'Are you... erm... going to sit?'

*Ah... so she was a mind reader. That was bad news!*

'Sit? Yes, good plan,' he muttered, feeling increasingly awkward – though he wasn't entirely sure why.

Maybe it had something to do with the fact that the object of his desire had turned up out of nowhere, been naked in his shower, and was now sitting in his kitchen, wearing his clothes. *Or* maybe it was because they'd only shared about five words before the most memorable kiss of his life... and then not spoken again for a year and a half.

'You're looking a bit pale,' she said with a worried frown.

'Didn't sleep too well in hospital,' he mumbled,

scrunching his eyes closed in an attempt to make the room stay still. It didn't help. He quickly sank down into the chair opposite Milly. Better to sit down before he fell down, after all!

'I bet,' said Milly, shooting him a look that was both sympathetic and – for some reason – full of guilt. She pulled her coffee towards her and cradled it in her hands.

'Are you cold?' he said.

'I'm fine, thanks,' said Milly, shaking her head. 'But seriously though – are you okay? After the... erm... accident, I mean.'

'I'm fine,' he sighed.

'That's not what everyone's been saying and I've been so worried!' she said, her words tripping over themselves. 'That's why I'm here, in case you're wondering. I wanted to apologise.'

'What on earth for?' said Murray, raising his eyebrows – then wishing he hadn't. That *hurt!* 'And... what's everyone saying?'

He wasn't sure he really wanted to know... but perhaps it was better coming from Milly than finding out the next time Josh left an obnoxious message on his answering machine.

'I'm sorry about the flowers,' said Milly, scrubbing at her face. 'I mean – I know how heavy that bouquet was. It's what Elizabeth wanted... but they should have come with a health and safety warning or something and...'

Murray held up a hand and shook his head. 'Milly – seriously,' he chuckled, 'there's no way it was your fault.'

'But I—'

'Nope!' said Murray, cutting across her.

'The flowers—'

'Nope!' said Murray again.

Milly's worried expression morphed into a grin, and for a second Murray basked in the fact that he'd put that smile on her beautiful face.

'Okay then,' she said. 'Well… thanks. And I *am* sorry you got hurt. Bet you'll be forever traumatised by the sight of hand-tied flowers after that!'

'Honestly?' said Murray. 'I don't remember much about it.'

'Huh. Well… brace yourself for a few different versions because most of the town's talking about it,' said Milly.

'They are?' he said on a groan. It shouldn't really surprise him, given Brian's report about the whole thing in the taxi earlier on.

'Yep. In fact – several of them are hunting for your missing teeth like they're some kind of weird-ass trophy,' said Milly. 'Makes me think of those serial-killer documentaries!'

'My teeth?' said Murray in confusion.

'There's a rumour going around they got knocked out when you went down!' she said, scrunching up her nose. 'Jo – my trainee – asked if she could have a longer lunch break to join the hunt for them.'

'Gross!' chuckled Murray. 'Also pointless. No teeth were harmed in the making of this disaster.'

'Really?' said Milly.

'Yep,' he said, giving her a wide toothy grin to prove the point.

'Well... that's something,' said Milly. 'And no blood?'

'Nope,' said Murray. 'Just a slightly disappointing bump on my head and a great big dollop of embarrassment.'

'Don't be embarrassed,' said Milly. 'It's not like it was your fault!'

'Erm... well... it is a little bit,' he said.

'How?' demanded Milly.

'I was distracted,' he muttered.

'Right... well, it *was* very busy,' said Milly.

Murray nodded and sighed. He should stop talking. He'd already made a big enough prat out of himself in front of her. He didn't need to confirm the levels he was prepared to stoop to when she was around, did he?!

But then... she was sitting right there in front of him.

He might as well own up to the full, excruciating truth of the situation while he had her undivided attention. After all, he had to face facts – he'd probably never get the chance to talk to her again after this. Why would someone like *her* want anything to do with *him*?!

'I wasn't paying attention because I was looking for you,' he said bluntly.

'Me?' said Milly, clearly surprised.

'Yes... in the crowd.'

*Why? Why couldn't he have just let this go?*

'Oh,' said Milly.

'In fact,' he said, preparing himself for abject humiliation, 'you were pretty much the only reason I agreed to have anything to do with the wedding.'

'Me?' she said again, shaking her head slightly.

'You,' he agreed. 'I knew you were doing the flowers, and I knew you'd been invited. I wanted to see you... again. After... well... I don't know if you remember but... again.'

*He was making a real pig's ear out of this, wasn't he?*

Murray paused and cleared his throat. Poor woman. She was going to leg it off the trawler before she'd even drunk her coffee if he wasn't careful. Mud be damned!

'Anyway,' he said, 'it didn't work out quite the way I'd planned.'

'What did you have planned?' she said quietly.

'I was hoping we might at least get to dance,' he said, feeling his face grow hot as he met her eyes. 'Instead, I got to ride in the back of an ambulance... and I don't even remember it. If only I'd stayed inside and gone over my speech, none of it would have happened. Maybe we'd have...'

Murray trailed off. He'd said way too much already.

Milly was now fidgeting in her chair and picking at the handle of her coffee cup.

Great, he'd made her feel uncomfortable.

This was why he'd left it so ridiculously long to talk to her again. Why he'd never summoned the courage to do something about his monumental crush. To say he wasn't good at small talk was an understatement.

Letting out a sigh of defeat, Murray hauled himself out of the chair again and headed back to the coffee machine. He didn't really want another drink… but it was better than sitting in awkward silence across from Milly while he waited for her look of mild confusion to morph into one of horror.

'You *are* kidding me… right?'

Milly's voice made him turn in surprise. She had a strange look on her face. Quizzical… but definitely not horrified. In fact, she looked like she was caught somewhere between surprise… laughter and… hope?

'Kidding about what?' he said, wondering if maybe those flowers had done more damage than the scans had revealed. What if this was one of the side effects they'd told him to look out for – a hallucination, perhaps? Maybe the girl of his dreams – sitting in his kitchen, wearing his clothes after taking a shower in his bathroom – was just a figment of his imagination. A symptom of a good thrashing by a bunch of daisies.

It certainly seemed a lot more plausible than Milly rowing all the way out to the trawler to check he was okay. Of course, if she *was* just a phantom who was about to disappear in a puff of smoke, it would be safe to tell her. After just one kiss, he'd fallen in love with her - a perfect stranger.

'Earth to Murray!' said the phantom gently.

'Huh?" he mumbled, swaying on the spot.

'Murray?' the phantom got to her feet, looking a bit freaked out. 'I think you'd better sit down!'

CHAPTER 13

MILLY

Milly grabbed Murray's arm as he wobbled precariously.

'Come on,' she said, worry lacing her voice. 'You need to sit down!'

Wrapping one arm around his waist, she held on tightly as she guided him back towards his chair. She watched in concern as he sank down onto it.

*Was his head bothering him?*

He'd been perfectly fine… until suddenly, he wasn't. The colour had drained from his face, and for a moment she'd been convinced he was about to faint.

Milly's guilt about turning up at Murray's place unannounced promptly disappeared. There was no way he should be all the way out here on his own right now. Even if the hospital *had* booted him out, something clearly wasn't quite right.

Staring down at him as he swayed gently on the

chair, Milly wondered what she could do to help. Should she call the doctor or something?

Other than wincing slightly when he'd run his fingers through his hair earlier, Murray had seemed to be well enough. Now, though? He definitely *wasn't* well. In fact, he looked a bit like she did when she forgot to take a lunch break.

*Ah!*

'Murray?' she said gently, watching as he tried to prop his head up with both hands.

'Mmm?'

'When did you last have something to eat?'

'Eat?' he echoed, looking confused, as though the concept of food was completely alien.

'Yeah – you know… breakfast? Or lunch?' said Milly.

'I… actually, I have no idea,' said Murray. 'Maybe… teatime.'

'Teatime?' gasped Milly. 'You mean you haven't eaten anything since yesterday?'

'Maybe?' said Murray, rubbing his eyes.

'Okay, well… that's probably part of the problem,' she said, heading for the doorway.

'Are you going?' said Murray, looking confused as he started to rise from his chair.

'You wish,' she chuckled. 'I'm just going to grab my bag, and then I'm making you some food.'

'But… you don't have to…'

'Sit!' she said as he wobbled again.

Changing direction, Milly dashed over to him and placed her hands on his shoulders. Gently but firmly, she forced him back down into his chair. She knew it wasn't her place to order him around in his own home, but it was either that or end up with an unconscious heap of Murray Eddington to deal with – and there was no way she was about to risk it!

'Stay put a sec,' she commanded, then darted from the room.

It took a couple of seconds to locate her shopping bag on the floor next to the sofa. It was mercifully mud-free, and the knot she'd tied in the handles had kept everything safe and sound during her rescue from the marshes.

'Mind if I see what you've got in the fridge?' she said, striding back through to the kitchen and breathing a sigh of relief to find Murray still slumped in his chair. He'd rested his elbows on the table, and his face was in his hands.

Milly dumped her bag onto the counter and then opened the fridge before Murray had the chance to formulate a reply. It was remarkably well-stocked. There were plenty of veggies, fresh mushrooms, a box of eggs, milk…

'I don't have any bread,' said Murray. 'I was going to make some later… but…'

'No need – I dashed into the bakery on my way down the hill,' said Milly, feeling triumphant that at least one of the decisions she'd made today had been the right one. 'I wasn't sure if you'd have the basics when you got back from the hospital, and I didn't think you'd want the hassle of heading back into town again…'

Milly trailed off. Just the fact that she was there meant that he had no choice in the matter. If he wanted to get rid of her, he'd *have* to head out again. Milly's boat was stuck in the mud, and she wouldn't be able to get back to Crumbleton without Murray's help. Looking at the state of him right now, though, he wouldn't be going anywhere any time soon.

'You brought me bread?' he said, blinking at her and looking adorably befuddled and sleepy.

'Yeah,' she said. 'And a small bottle of milk, a couple of slices of cake-'

'Cake?' he said, perking up.

Milly smiled. 'Lemon drizzle, chocolate rice crispy and a cherry flapjack.'

'My favourite!' said Murray.

'Which one?' said Milly.

'All of them,' said Murray.

'Well… that's good,' she laughed. 'That can be pudding. And how do you feel about cheese toasties?'

'Strongly pro,' said Murray, his face serious.

'Or I can make you an omelette?' said Milly.

'You had me at cheese toasties,' said Murray. 'I'll help—'

'Nope!' said Milly. 'Just tell me where you keep your cheese grater and I'll do the rest. I *would* suggest you go and grab that second shower... but I think you'd better stay put until you've had something to eat.'

～

'Best. Toasties. Ever.' Murray popped the last bite into his mouth and sat back in his chair, his eyes closed and a happy little smile playing around his lips as he chewed.

Milly couldn't help but echo that smile – though she was grateful he had his eyes closed for a moment because she couldn't seem to look away from him.

The food had worked its magic, and the colour had come back to Murray's cheeks. It was as though the fragrant, fatty goodness had breathed life back into him - which was a huge relief. Milly wasn't really sure how to call a doctor out to a stranded trawler in the middle of the marshes!

'Better?' she said gently.

Considering Murray had just demolished an entire mountain of cheese toasties, she had a feeling she knew the answer to that question already. She'd helped herself to one when he'd insisted that she joined him – but Milly hadn't got much of a look in after that. The man had clearly been starving and had wolfed the food down with little moans that had made her blush.

'I feel like a new man,' he said, opening his eyes again and beaming a smile at her that made her tingle from her head to her toes. 'Thank you. And... just for the record... I don't normally go all weak and feeble and expect my dates to cook emergency toasties!'

Milly swallowed. *A date – is that what this was?* She decided to let that one lie. She didn't want to make him feel "weak and feeble" again! Hadn't he already admitted that he'd been at the wedding just to see her? But... he'd been on the verge of passing out at that point, so it didn't seem fair to take anything he'd said *too* seriously.

'Okay,' she said. 'Noted.'

'Not that this is a date of course!' he said, suddenly looking horrified. 'God, I don't know what's wrong with me today. Just... ignore everything I've said since you got here!'

'Everything?' said Milly, a lump of congealed disappointment landing in her stomach.

'Maybe,' he said.

'It would be a bit of a shame,' she said lightly. 'To forget everything, I mean. You said you went to the wedding to – erm – see me?'

Murray squirmed slightly. She felt a bit mean bringing it back up – but she couldn't face another eighteen months of pining. She might as well come clean. After all – it might be the only chance she got.

'That's why I went to the wedding too... to speak to you. Or... I don't know... to see you – and dance with you?'

'Am I hallucinating again?' said Murray faintly.

Milly grinned at him. 'Don't think so…? Unless I'm a purple dinosaur or something?'

'Definitely *not* a purple dinosaur,' he laughed.

'Well, that's something,' she replied.

'And you're definitely here?' said Murray.

Milly nodded, and then – before she could overthink it – she reached out and laid her hand over his on the tabletop. 'I'm definitely here,' she agreed, squeezing slightly.

'Oh,' said Murray, his eyes on hers.

They both fell silent, and Milly removed her hand before things could get weird.

*Hah! Bit late for that!*

'Want a piece of cake?' she said.

'I want all the cake,' laughed Murray. 'And more coffee.'

'And then…?' said Milly, wondering how to broach the subject of getting home. After all, he seemed to be fine again, and she didn't want to outstay her welcome… any more than she already had just by turning up!

'Then?' said Murray, turning to her with a gleam in his eye. 'Then I think we should go to bed.'

*What?!*

Milly felt her jaw drop. She blinked once. Twice.

*Had he really just said that?*

'B-bed?' she stammered.

Murray grinned at her. There was no trace of his previous discombobulation now.

'I don't know about you,' he said, mildly, 'but I'm going to need a nap after all the excitement. Would you care to join me?'

*A nap? Was it her turn to start hallucinating? Maybe she really was a purple dinosaur.*

A slow smile spread over Milly's face – which promptly morphed into an embarrassingly enthusiastic yawn. What was it about the word nap? It was almost like it created a chemical reaction that induced sleepiness.

'I don't mind chilling on your sofa for a bit while you grab a nap,' she said.

'The sofa's too short for a decent nap,' he said, not taking his eyes off her. 'Trust me – I've tested it several times. Anyway – it's a big bed.'

Milly shrugged. *Why not?* This had already been the weirdest afternoon she'd had in a *very* long time. Why shouldn't she join him for a quick snooze on that giant bed of his? After all – at least she'd be able to keep half an eye on him.

'Okay,' she said. 'Let's nap.'

## CHAPTER 14

MURRAY

Murray yawned widely as he made his way back out on deck. Despite downing yet another cup of coffee and sharing a nibble of all three types of cake Milly had brought with her, he was still struggling to fully surface from his nap. He'd never slept so well in his life... which was a miracle, considering what a weird situation he'd managed to land himself in.

The *idea* of sharing a nap with Milly had been inspired. The reality was *far* more awkward than he'd anticipated. Or at least it was to start with!

He'd lain there on his back, frozen to the spot – more than aware that she was just a foot away, doing exactly the same thing. He'd pulled the duvet over both of them and they'd gone completely still – not saying a word to each other – as if the downy cover had cast some kind of spell over them.

Murray had never been so aware of how loud his breathing was - and had promptly tried to do it more quietly… which had only served to make his heart race. He was just starting to give up on the idea of sleeping at all - even though he was so exhausted he felt like an elephant was sitting on his head - when he felt Milly start to drop off next to him.

Her breathing became slow and steady, and her entire body seemed to sink a little into the mattress as sleep stole over her. That had been his own cue, and he'd finally let himself drift off with a huge smile on his face.

Murray had to admit, opening his eyes to find Milly Rowlands still dozing right next to him had practically been a religious experience. The pair of them had snuggled up to each other in their sleep, and he was close enough to count every golden freckle that dusted the bridge of her nose. He was close enough that he could have kissed her.

He didn't, of course – and he'd been kicking himself for that ever since. Murray liked to think of himself as a gentleman, though. Asking someone if they wanted to share your afternoon nap was one thing. Pouncing on them when they were enjoying said nap was another thing entirely.

Still, when Milly opened her eyes and stared dreamily at him as if she was trying to figure out if he was real or not, it had taken every ounce of his resolve not to wrap his arms around her and close that last little gap between them.

Murray couldn't help but feel like he'd somehow missed a golden opportunity. Maybe the only opportunity he'd get to show her how he felt about her. He'd tried to tell her... but then he'd almost passed out, so that definitely hadn't gone to plan!

'You okay?' said Milly, bringing him back to his senses as she followed him onto the deck and closed the trawler door softly behind her. 'Are you sure you're up for this? You were miles away there for a moment!'

'Yeah, I'm fine,' said Murray, smiling at her. 'And I'm definitely up for it. I feel like a new man after sleep and cake and coffee. Besides, I think I owe you one after everything you've done for me!'

'What, like turning up uninvited and then screaming your name until you came to my rescue because I got stuck in the mud?' she laughed.

'Like bringing me groceries,' countered Murray.

'Like stealing your hot water, using your shower gel and helping myself from your wardrobe?' said Milly.

'Like making me lunch and then making sure I didn't die in my sleep!' said Murray with a wry smile.

'Okay, you win,' chuckled Milly.

'Good,' said Murray. 'Anyway, it won't take me half a minute to row you back into town.'

'Well... thank you,' said Milly. 'For the nap, and the water-taxi... and not making me feel like a total loser for just turning up.'

Murray shrugged, and she smiled at him. The butterflies in his stomach swooped into action yet again.

If he was being honest, he didn't *really* want to take her back. Not because he wasn't feeling up to it – but because he simply didn't want her to leave. Milly was easy company. She was fun, thoughtful, and ridiculously beautiful in her borrowed clothes.

But... he'd already more than pushed the boundaries of what was acceptable for a first date. *Not* that this was a date, of course. Still - in his befuddled, post-food exhaustion, he'd basically held her hostage by demanding a nap. He couldn't exactly ask her to stay even longer, could he? No – it was best if he took her home now before the effects of the nap started to wear off and he got all idiotic again.

'Here,' he said, holding her shopping bag out towards her. 'I folded your muddy clothes and put them in there for you.'

'You did?' she said, looking surprised.

'Yeah,' he said. 'I hope that was alright?'

'You're a keeper, Murray Eddington,' she said, grinning at him.

Murray cleared his throat. He didn't really know what to say to that... other than beg for her phone number or ask her on a date – a *proper* date. Unfortunately, the weird bout of bravery that had come over him when he'd been addled by painkillers and high on cheese toasties seemed to have worn off.

'Let's get this show on the road!' he said. Then he turned away from her and grimaced.

*What a prat - he sounded like a game show host. Or the embarrassing uncle at a wedding!*

If Milly had noticed his unease, she didn't show it. She practically bounced along behind him as he led the way to his rowing boat. Then she settled herself comfortably on the seat while he untied it from the side of the trawler.

'Ready?' he said, sinking down opposite her.

'Always,' she replied with a grin.

*Another pang. Another swoop of butterflies.*

Murray quickly grabbed the oars and set off towards the spot where Milly's borrowed boat was still stranded.

Luckily, it didn't take too much effort to free the decrepit craft from its muddy prison. A loop of rope, some hefty nudging and a couple of well-chosen swearwords was all it took in the end.

'See – it just needed an expert pair of hands!' said Milly, as soon as he'd tied it to the back of his own boat so that they could tow it back to the wharf with them.

'I'm hardly an expert,' said Murray, rowing a few meters and then pausing again to fish out the oar Milly had lost overboard in her attempts to free herself.

'More of an expert than me, anyway,' said Milly with a shrug. 'Are you sure you don't want me to get back in and row myself home so you can head back and put your feet up?'

'No chance,' said Murray, settling himself opposite her again. There was no way he was about to relinquish these last few precious moments with her… especially as he might not get the chance to see her again. 'One rescue mission is more than enough for one day,' he added.

'Cheeky sod!' huffed Milly, prodding him with her foot.

Murray grinned, and they both fell silent as he headed for deeper water. A companionable kind of peace seemed to wrap around them as they drifted along, and Murray watched Milly as she gazed out across the marshes - lost in their tranquil beauty.

Murray knew he was biased, but it really was a magical place – especially bathed in evening sunlight, with the soft sound of the oars as they dipped in and out of the water creating a gentle lullaby. The sun was sliding towards the horizon, turning Crumbleton's hill with its castle on the top into a dreamy silhouette.

It felt like they reached the wharf in record time, and Murray didn't think he'd ever enjoyed the trip more. In fact, he could have kicked himself for not rowing a bit slower… or taking a slightly more scenic route - just to buy him a bit more time with Milly. It was too late for that now, though. They were back, and she was about to wander out of his life again. The thought made him feel a bit sick.

'You need a hand tying the other boat up?' said Milly, glancing behind them.

## FLOWERS GO FLYING IN CRUMBLETON

Murray shook his head. 'Nah, I'll sort that out when you're safely back ashore.'

He got to his feet, his heart sinking as he held out his hand to steady her. Milly climbed out of the boat and then paused on the stone steps.

This was goodbye… and he really didn't want it to be. It had been one of the weirdest days of his life… and one of the best, too.

'Thanks,' said Milly as she turned to smile down at him from her slightly higher vantage point.

'No problem,' said Murray. 'Oh – your bag.' He passed up the shopping bag full of muddy clothes. 'Well… bye then. And thanks for—'

'Hey Murray?'

Milly's voice cut across him, but he didn't mind. He didn't know what he'd been about to say anyway. He'd just been waffling in the vague hope of prolonging the moment.

'Yeah?' he said.

She beckoned for him to come closer, and he shuffled as near to the edge of the little boat as he dared. Milly leaned down and placed her hands on his shoulders. Before he knew what was happening, her soft mouth was on his.

*Was he hallucinating again?*

'I just wanted to say,' she said, looking slightly dazed as she pulled away from him, 'in case we don't get the chance to talk again - I thought you looked really nice wearing just a towel.'

Murray blinked, and Milly shot him a seriously cheeky smile.

This was his chance.

*Say something man!*

'Erm… thanks,' he spluttered.

*Smooth!*

He was reeling from the kiss – and a bit befuddled from everything else. It took him several seconds to realise that she was already walking away from him, giving him a little wave over her shoulder.

That had been his last chance to say something – to ask to see her again – and he'd blown it.

Murray stood stock still, watching as she sauntered towards the City Gates. Just before she was about to disappear from view, she turned around, gave him a salute and then blew him a kiss.

Murray smiled broadly as he returned the wave—and then she was gone.

'I don't even have your phone number!' he sighed.

But… he did know where her shop was, and this time, he wasn't going to rely on someone else's wedding to bring them back together. He was going to ask Milly Rowlands out on a date. A proper one - minus the mud and the dizzy spells.

## CHAPTER 15

### MILLY

*He was still watching! Was there anything better than that?!*

Milly waved like a lunatic. Then, turning reluctantly away from Murray, she practically skipped through the City Gates back into Crumbleton.

*She'd kissed him. She hadn't been able to stop herself!*

Goodness only knew what he thought of her after that... but if his dazed smile was anything to go by, and the fact that he'd watched her as she'd walked away...

*It had to be a good sign, right?!*

'Apart from the fact you still don't have his phone number—idiot!' she muttered, coming to an abrupt halt. She'd got so lost in the moment that it hadn't even crossed her mind. They hadn't arranged to see each other again either... and there was no way she'd be braving that boat trip again.

'Damnit!'

Milly loitered on the cobbles for a long moment, wondering what on earth she should do. She *could* just leave it up to fate and hope they'd bump into each other again. Maybe Murray would turn up at the shop...?

Well, one thing was for sure – she couldn't turn around and run back to the wharf to beg for his phone number... could she?

Nope. She had *some* pride.

Didn't she?

'Yes you do!' muttered Milly, forcing herself to carry on up the hill.

It had ended up being an unexpectedly lovely afternoon... almost romantic, in fact... if you didn't count Murray's head injury, of course! But in reality, were they any further forward than they'd been before her magical mystery tour of the marshes?

*Milly – you're officially overthinking things!*

'At least I know he's okay,' she sighed.

And she knew what his lips felt like on hers... and how beautiful he looked when he was wearing nothing more than a towel. Milly's daydreams were definitely in for an upgrade. That was the problem, though - daydreams were no longer going to cut it when it came to Murray Eddington. She liked him. She *more* than liked him. She wanted this to *go* somewhere!

Milly yanked her phone out of her pocket and checked the time. She'd completely lost track of the day after Murray had invited her to nap next to him in his

## FLOWERS GO FLYING IN CRUMBLETON

bed. Going by the fact that the sun had been practically kissing the horizon as he'd rowed her back across the marshes, she could only imagine that it was getting pretty late.

The phone screen sprang to life in her hand. Sure enough, it was long past closing time for the shop. Well – at least that meant she didn't have to hot-foot it to the top of the hill. Jo would have cashed up and locked up ages ago.

'Right then,' she muttered. 'Time to call Caroline!'

Her friend had made her promise to call the minute she got back into town to let her know what was really going on with Murray. That wasn't the reason Milly wanted to talk to her, though. Right now, she craved Caroline's particular brand of no-nonsense advice. With any luck, it might help her get her head back on straight – and figure out what she should do next.

Glancing around to make sure there was no one on the high street who might be inclined to eavesdrop, Milly pulled up Caroline's number.

'What happened?' said her friend the moment she picked up, completely dispensing with any of the usual greetings. 'You've been ages! Is he alive? Does he have all his teeth? Did you get to feel his bump?'

Milly let out a spluttering laugh. 'No, I did *not* get to feel his bump!'

'But something happened!' crowed Caroline.

'I didn't say that!' said Milly.

'You didn't have to,' said Caroline.

BETH RAIN

Milly was sure she just heard her friend's eyes roll.

'Why don't you come up to the office?' said Caroline.

'You're still at work?' said Milly in surprise.

'Kind of,' said Caroline. 'But I have wine!'

'I'll be there in five minutes.'

Three minutes and forty-five seconds later, Milly was thundering up the wooden staircase towards Caroline's little office at the Crumbleton Times and Echo.

'Wow, where's the fire?' laughed Caroline, as Milly burst in.

'You said you had wine!' said Milly with a grin.

Caroline had her feet propped up on her desk. She was busy clicking away with her computer mouse in one hand and nursing a half-drunk glass of wine in the other.

'I do have wine… but I'll deny it all if you blabber!' said Caroline with a naughty smile.

'As if I would,' said Milly. 'Besides, I can be bribed.'

'Thought that might be the case,' said Caroline, her feet hitting the deck as she sprang out of her chair to grab a second glass from the bookshelf behind her desk.

'Cheers!' said Milly, accepting the vat of red wine.

'Yeah, cheers!' said Caroline, watching her closely as she reached across the desk and clinked her glass against Milly's. 'Here's to whatever put that twinkle in your eye.'

'What?!' said Milly, blinking hard as though that might help. 'I don't have a twinkle, I don't even know what a twinkle is!'

'Uh-huh?' muttered Caroline, taking a disbelieving sip.

'Fine,' said Milly. 'Fine. It's true. *I'm twinkling.*'

'I *knew it!*' said Caroline, giving a celebratory fist pump. 'Tell me everything!'

'First things first,' said Milly, narrowing her eyes. 'Are you still writing that article about Murray's accident?'

'Well…' said Caroline, 'that all depends on what you're about to tell me.'

'Then I'm not telling you anything,' said Milly blandly. She could really do with offloading, but she wasn't going to risk it if there was a chance the rest of Crumbleton would be reading about it in the paper on Friday!

'Unclench, Mills!' chuckled Caroline. 'I was joking.'

'Oh,' said Milly.

'Yeah,' said Caroline rolling her eyes. 'Anyway – the answer's no. I'm not running the story.'

'You're not?' said Milly, trying not to look too pleased.

Caroline shook her head. 'Nah – I'd just got off the phone with the photographer when you called. She definitely didn't get a shot of it… and not a single one of those idiots with mobile phones managed to catch it either!'

'Shame,' said Milly lightly.

'Plus, your man hasn't called me back either,' said Caroline with a little huff.

'Not my man!' said Milly quickly.

'Uh-huh?' said Caroline again, raising her eyebrows curiously.

'So... the article's definitely been axed?' said Milly, trying to buy herself a couple more seconds to get her thoughts together.

'Yeah. It's a bit of a shame. Stuart from Bendall's has already themed his special offers for next week – hard hats, non-slip gloves and shin pads at half price!'

Milly let out a chuckle. 'Poor Stuart.'

'I'm sure he'll get over it,' said Caroline. 'Anyway, I'm pretty sure the Dolphin and Anchor will be glad it's not running – I don't think they've been enjoying the unexpected publicity as it is. Apparently, they've had to start throwing people out of their carpark. According to my sources, they were there looking for teeth?!'

'Yeah. Jo went down there on her lunch break,' said Milly.

'Hey – Mills?' said Caroline, narrowing her eyes.

'Yeah?' said Milly, bracing herself.

'What on *Earth* are you wearing?' said Caroline.

Milly glanced down at Murray's oversized man-shorts, and his soft cotton tee shirt peeping out from the V-neck of her jumper... and smiled.

'And what's that smile?!' demanded Caroline, her eyes gleaming with curiosity.

'What smile?' said Milly – rather pointlessly considering she was grinning so widely that she was at risk of pulling one of her cheek muscles. 'And the clothes are a long story,' she added.

'I've got time,' said Caroline with a little shrug. 'But – first things first – is Murray okay?'

'Yeah,' said Milly, feeling her smile stretch wider still. She probably looked like a love-sick teenager by this point.

'Urgh, wait! If you're going to be all cute about it...' said Caroline. Holding up her hand for Milly to stop talking, she reached for the bottle of wine and topped off her own glass before doing the same to Milly's. Then she took a deep swig. 'Okay – I'm ready.'

'He's fine,' said Milly.

'All teeth accounted for?' said Caroline.

'Yep. And no blood,' said Milly. 'He's not been back from hospital for long, though. Sounds like he got a pretty nasty bump on the head – and I bet there was a bit of concussion. But, other than being a bit all over the place because he'd forgotten to eat... he seemed to be okay.'

Milly stopped talking and took a sip of her wine. Caroline just sat there, watching her.

'What?' said Milly after several long seconds.

'Is that it?' said Caroline, looking disappointed. 'You said it was a long story. That wasn't even worth cracking out the emergency office wine!'

'To be fair,' said Milly, 'you had that open before I even called.'

'Damn... you weren't meant to remember that bit!' laughed Caroline. 'But seriously... what's with you? The smiling... the twinkles...? I *know* something else must have happened. According to Jo, you've been gone all afternoon.'

'Ooh, she's soooo fired,' muttered Milly.

'And you haven't told me why you're wearing those!' Caroline continued, pointing at Murray's shorts.

'I happen to like them,' said Milly mildly.

'And I happen to know they're not yours,' countered Caroline. 'Come on, out with it!'

Milly took a deep breath. 'Off the record?!'

'Of course,' tutted Caroline. 'As if you have to ask!'

'Well then,' said Milly, 'it's like this...'

She had to hand it to Caroline – she made an excellent audience. She groaned and cheered and gasped in all the right places... and she even let out a little sigh when Milly told her about the kiss.

'So – you *did* get to feel his bump!' said Caroline with a teasing grin. 'I knew it!'

'Get your mind out of the gutter, Car!' huffed Milly. 'It was all very sweet, and lovely, and innocent.'

'Oh *yeah* – super innocent!' said Caroline, rolling her eyes. 'Tell me that bit about you ogling him in a towel again.'

Milly smirked, but after a couple of seconds, it slid right off her face.

'What?' said Caroline. 'Did reality not quite live up to eighteen months of fantasising?'

'It's not that. It *more* than lived up to it!' she sighed. 'It's just… I don't have his phone number.'

'You're kidding me,' said Caroline. 'You spent a whole afternoon with the guy… you slept with him—'

'*Next* to him!' Milly cut in.

'Same difference,' shrugged Caroline.

'*Really* not!' insisted Milly.

'Whatever. You slept on his boat… and now you're telling me you have no way of contacting him?'

'Pretty much,' said Milly, feeling a bit sheepish. 'I was caught up in the moment.'

'Uh-huh?' said Caroline. 'Did you at least arrange to see him again?'

Milly gave her head a tiny shake. 'Nope.'

'Dumbass,' said Caroline affectionately.

'I know,' said Milly.

'Well – I've got his number,' said Caroline with a little shrug.

'You do?' said Milly, her eyes going wide as she did her best to resist making grabby hands across the desk.

'Of course,' said Caroline. 'I got it from the Dolphin and Anchor earlier so that I could call him about the article.'

'Can I…?' said Milly.

'Nope,' said Caroline, smiling at her benignly. 'I

can't go giving out contact information for my sources willy-nilly, Milly! Imagine if that got out. I'm a professional, after all.' She grinned and then took a theatrical sip of wine.

'But—' started Milly.

'Of course, I *could* call him for you,' she said. 'Maybe give him your phone number?'

Milly stared at her for a long moment. 'Won't that make me look a bit… desperate?'

'*Aren't* you a bit desperate?' said Caroline.

'Oi!' squeaked Milly.

'About him, I mean,' said Caroline. 'Not in general.'

'I don't know, Car,' said Milly. 'It could backfire…'

'What, like getting stuck in the middle of Crumbleton marshes and having to get rescued?' said Caroline. 'That kind of backfiring, you mean?'

Milly cocked her head. 'Okay – fair point. I'm sold. Do it!'

'Ooh, fun!' said Caroline, grabbing a post-it note from the wall and pulling the phone towards her.

## CHAPTER 16

### MURRAY

Murray still had an idiotic grin plastered across his face as he tied the boat securely back to the side of the trawler, and then heaved himself aboard. Gone was the headache. Gone was the intense desire to sleep for a week. Milly Rowlands really was some kind of miracle cure for a bash on the head.

Strolling across the deck, Murray sucked in a deep breath of evening air, then turned to stare out at the marshes, golden and gleaming under the lowering sun. The birdsong sounded sweeter than usual, and he had a horrible feeling… a wonderful feeling… was he falling…?

The sound of the Sat Phone rent the air, breaking the spell. Murray groaned. That was going to be Josh again, wasn't it? The idiot really didn't get the message easily. If you ignored most people long enough, they simply went away, but Josh was tenacious.

Rolling his eyes, he strode for the cabin. He knew better than to ignore the call. If it *was* Josh, he'd just keep ringing every five minutes for all eternity – or until Murray answered. He couldn't be dealing with that tonight. He wanted to revel in the incredible, unexpected, wonderful day he'd just had.

Milly had kissed him – again.

'What?' he said, yanking the phone out of its cradle and pressing it against his ear.

'Don't say *what* like that, Murray Eddington!'

Murray flinched. It was a woman's voice. Stern and no-nonsense. It simultaneously made him think of his mum and the scary dinner lady he'd had at primary school.

'Erm... sorry... hello?' he said, trying to place who it was.

'Hi!' said the voice again, and this time, there was a bubble of laughter behind it. 'It's Caroline Cook from the Crumbleton Times and Echo.'

Of *course* it was!

'Oh... right,' said Murray, slumping slightly. At least it wasn't Josh, but Caroline wasn't much better. He didn't fancy getting grilled about the humiliation of Saturday. 'Sorry I didn't call you back. I—'

'Don't worry about that,' said Caroline. 'I've dropped the story. You'll probably be pleased to hear that I can't get a decent photograph of the whole thing for love nor money. In fact – I can't get *any* kind of photo of it!'

'Erm... well...' Murray realised his grin was back in place. 'I'm sorry to hear that.'

'No you're not!' hooted Caroline.

'Okay – you're right,' said Murray. 'So... to what do I owe the pleasure?'

'I'm calling to ask you out on a date,' said Caroline.

Murray's jaw dropped, but in his stunned silence, he heard a strange squawk on the other end of the line.

'Erm... you okay?' he said. It sounded a bit like Caroline had just walked into a wall.

'She's fine!' came a different voice.

'Gimmie that!' said Caroline again, sounding muffled and somehow further away.

'Murray?'

'I'm still here?' said Murray, giving himself a little pinch just to check he hadn't fallen into some kind of weird dream. That voice sounded strangely like Milly.

'Aha! Unhand my phone, you blaggard!'

Caroline's yell made Murray ease the handset away from his ear, and a great deal of scuffling and half-strangled giggling erupted on the other end.

'Hello? Murray my man, are you still there?' Caroline was huffing and puffing now, but clearly back in control of the phone.

'I am,' he said. 'Do you need some kind of... assistance?'

'Assistance?' chuckled Caroline. 'Nah – your

girlfriend's been picking fights with me and losing since primary school.'

'Girlfriend?'

Murray's voice had just shot out of him in a squeak of surprise – and he heard it echoed on the other end by an equally loud yelp.

'Not... you suck, Caroline... I'm going to kill... and then... wine... git!'

Murray grinned. He might not have been able to make out the entire muffled sentence, but that voice was unmistakably Milly's.

'Is she okay?' he said cautiously.

'Yes,' said Caroline. 'She just doesn't like it when I sit on her.'

Murray snorted.

'Anyway, as I was saying before I was so rudely interrupted...'

*Giggle... squeak...*

'Shh woman!' grunted Caroline. 'Your *girlfriend* had her brains addled so badly by snogging you, she forgot to ask you for your phone number. I had it – but because I'm a professional—'

'Don't listen to her, she's got wine!' interrupted Milly before breaking into a round of violent giggles that made Murray suspect she was being tickled into silence.

'Lies, all lies!' said Caroline blithely. The fact that she'd slurred the word both times made Murray promptly side with Milly. 'Anyway – I couldn't just give her your number, could I?'

'You couldn't?' said Murray, struggling to keep a straight face.

'No chance,' she said. 'Where's the fun in that!'

'Erm… well… can I talk to her now?' he said.

Caroline went quiet for a moment. 'Okay, fine.'

Murray could almost hear her pout.

'Murray?' came Milly's voice.

'Yeah… hi?' he said. 'You okay?'

'Yeah,' said Milly. She sounded like she was smiling. 'Caroline weighs a ton.'

'Meanie!' came Caroline's voice in the background.

'So…' said Murray, suddenly lost for words now that he had Milly on the line.

'So… how are you?' said Milly.

'Oh for goodness sake!' said Caroline. There was another round of scuffling and the phone beeped.

'Erm – you still there?' said Murray.

'This is Caroline,' said Caroline. 'See – that's exactly why I didn't let her call in the first place. I knew we'd be here until Christmas just waiting for the pair of you to say something useful. Your girlfriend wants to ask you on a proper date.'

'I didn't—' squeaked Milly.

'You hush!' said Caroline, using her scary dinner lady voice again. 'Murray you've got three choices. Hotel, Milly's place or your place.'

'Not the hotel!' said Murray quickly. Somehow, he didn't think he'd be heading back there for a while.

'Not his place,' came Milly's voice. 'I'm crap at rowing!'

'Right,' said Caroline. 'Milly will cook dinner for you tomorrow night. Be there at six-thirty.'

'I can do that,' said Murray.

'I can't cook,' said Milly.

'So go to the bakery for some pasties and pretend!' huffed Caroline. 'Murray,' she added, turning her attention back to him, 'dress smart!'

'I'm not wearing a suit,' said Murray.

'Tell him to wear his towel!'

'Milly says to wear your—'

'Yeah, I heard,' chuckled Murray.

'And don't even think about bringing her flowers,' said Caroline. 'She likes cola cubes, though!'

The line went dead.

Murray stared at the handset for a long moment. He had a date with Milly. A proper date. Sure, Caroline hadn't actually given him her phone number… but he'd be able to rectify that when he saw her tomorrow. It would be the first thing he did. Okay - maybe the third thing. First, he'd hand over a huge bag of cola cubes, second, he'd kiss her… *then* he'd get her number.

'Sounds like a plan!' he said to himself with a determined little nod, which belied the tangle of nerves already expanding in his stomach. He was just about to replace the handset when it started ringing again.

## FLOWERS GO FLYING IN CRUMBLETON

'Hello?' he said, his heart pumping, a broad smile spreading on his face as he prepared himself for another round of the Caroline and Milly show.

'Mate. It's Josh. So – what did you think of my speech? Genius, right?'

∼

Murray was nervous. So nervous that he decided against taking the winding, uneven steps that led to the top of Crumbleton. Sure, it was tempting to take the back route up to Milly's flat, but the last thing he needed right now was for his legs to give way. Face-planting into the uneven stone and turning up bruised, bleeding and missing a tooth or two definitely wasn't the look he was going for.

He was determined that this date was going to go well – preferably without a head injury, an ambulance, a ton of marsh mud or the need for a restorative nap partway through.

*Actually... the nap part wouldn't be so bad!*

Murray grinned to himself as he ambled slowly up the cobbles past the little courtyard in front of the Crumbleton Times and Echo offices. He might not be taking Milly any flowers... but if tonight went well, he'd definitely be sending some down to Caroline!

Murray blew out a long, slow breath, doing his best to calm his racing heart – which had nothing to do with the steep hill and everything to do with the woman waiting for him at the top of it.

Taking Caroline's advice, Murray had already done a lap of the shops. He'd arrived in town early to grab a large paper bag full of cola cubes from the sweet shop. Then, deciding that it wasn't nearly enough of an offering, he'd nipped into the bakery and added a whole cherry Madeira cake and half a dozen chocolate brownies to his haul.

Being in town hadn't been as bad as he'd feared. He'd half-expected a barrage of questions about what had happened at the wedding. Instead, all he'd been met with was genuine concern and several offers of help. Stuart from Bendall's had even volunteered to deliver supplies all the way out to the trawler if he ever needed him to. Murray had been touched – especially when Stuart had then insisted on gifting him a vat of salted caramel ice cream to "help him feel better". He couldn't wait to dollop it on top of a brownie and share it with Milly.

The combination of ice cream and Milly in the same thought made Murray's knees wobble dangerously, and he sucked in another deep breath. He didn't know why he was being so ridiculous – Milly's visit to the trawler hadn't exactly been under the most romantic of circumstances. She'd already seen him at his worst – and yet, she'd been easy, lovely company. There was no reason tonight should be any different.

*Except that this is officially a date!*

## FLOWERS GO FLYING IN CRUMBLETON

The thought prodded him in the back of the brain and his heart suddenly felt like it was going to explode out of his chest. But... it was only *officially* a date because that's what Caroline had called it. In reality, it was just two people meeting up to eat half the contents of the Crumbleton Bakery.

Yes. That's what they were doing. Brownies and ice cream and chat. That wasn't scary at all... was it?!

*Knock you idiot - you're already there!*

Murray blinked. He was standing outside of Milly's flat. He'd just marched up the high street on autopilot and reached the door next to the flower shop without even thinking about it.

Raising his hand, Murray knocked quickly before he had the chance to get cold feet and chicken out of the whole thing. Not that he could of course - because he didn't have Milly's number and there was no way he'd just disappear on her!

Thundering footsteps from the other side of the door echoed his rowdy heartbeat. Before he could arrange his face into anything other than a dorky smile, the door flew open, and she was standing right in front of him.

'Milly!' he said. It was the only thing he could think to say.

'Damn,' she said with a frown.

Murray's eyebrows shot up. That wasn't quite the greeting he'd been hoping for.

'What?' he said.

'You're not wearing the towel!'

Murray relaxed and grinned at her. 'No – but I do have cola cubes, ice cream and way more cake than is good for us,' he said, raising the shopping bag slightly.

'I like your style, Murray Eddington,' she said. 'Come on up!'

## CHAPTER 17

### MILLY

'Yo! Boss... you're doing that thing again!'

'Huh? What thing?' said Milly vaguely, turning to blink at Jo.

*When had her trainee snuck up on her?!*

'You know – that thing where you stand with the shop keys in your hand and don't actually use them to unlock,' huffed Jo.

'Right,' said Milly. 'Right... sorry.'

With one last peek at the door of her flat, she did her best to pull herself together... and to quell the smug smile that was threatening to sneak onto her face while she was at it.

Popping the key into the lock, Milly opened the door and made the usual dash for the alarm. She needed to get Jo inside before the girl had the chance to twig that she was hiding something. Or – in this case - *someone*.

'Okay, let's get this show on the road!' said Milly, re-emerging and rubbing her hands together.

'Urgh – you're far too perky for this time in the morning, especially considering we haven't done the coffee run yet,' grumbled Jo. She shrugged out of her red jacket with its line of silver military buttons to reveal a pair of sunflower dungarees underneath. 'What's with you, anyway?'

'I'm high on life,' said Milly. 'And on that note - your dungarees…'

'Ah maaaan!' whined Jo. 'I'm wearing my staff top underneath – see?' She tugged at the pink collar.

'Uh-huh?' said Milly, raising an eyebrow.

'And I chose them because they're themed!' said Jo. 'Who wouldn't want to buy flowers from a florist covered from head to toe in sunflowers?'

Milly cocked her head, then stared down at her own pale pink polo shirt that she was wearing over a pair of neat – and stupendously boring - jeans.

'What?' said Jo. 'You're looking mad. Not angry-mad… nutso-mad.'

'I just think… you might be right,' said Milly slowly.

'Hold the phone, what's that now?' said Jo, peering around the shop with her hand cupped theatrically to one ear. 'Damnit – there were no witnesses!'

'Haha, very funny!' said Milly, looking her trainee up and down again. Jo looked vibrant and quirky. 'You do look amazing, though. You've inspired me. Maybe it's time for a new staff dress code.'

'Oh yeah?' said Jo, her eyes lighting up. 'Like what?'

Milly pointed at Jo's dungarees. 'Flowers. And fun. And colour.'

'I like it!' said Jo.

'But when we make deliveries – we'll still have to wear the polos.'

'They're so boring, though,' said Jo, wrinkling her nose. 'No offence! But, wouldn't it be better to have something that set us apart a bit?'

'Any suggestions?' said Milly.

'Embroidered denim jackets!' said Jo. 'Or… oh I know… remember those jackets the Pink Ladies wear in Grease? But with *Milly's Flowers* on them instead - maybe highlighted with a funky, swirly, floral design that looks a bit like a tattoo?'

'Sold!' said Milly. 'I love it. I always wanted to be a Pink Lady.'

Jo narrowed her eyes at her again and Milly cocked her head. 'What?'

'You're… different,' she said. 'I can't put my finger on it.'

'Just make the most of it!' said Milly with a grin.

'Okay – how about a raise?' said Jo, doing her best to look innocent and failing miserably.

'How about we re-visit that when your buttonholes don't disintegrate five minutes after you've made them?' countered Milly.

'Deal!' said Jo. 'Right, shall I get coffees now or…?

'Erm… not sure,' said Milly, glancing out of the

window and then trying to hide it by staring hard at the order pad next to the till.

'What's going on?!' said Jo.

'Nothing... I... nothing...' said Milly, racking her brain.

'Spit it out, young lady!' said Jo, crossing her arms.

Milly snorted. 'Did you just *young lady* me?!'

'Well, someone's got to!' said Jo. 'Sorry,' she added, not sounding in the least bit sorry.

'It's just... I... the windows,' said Milly. It was something she'd been meaning to talk to Jo about since the weekend – and right now it might just help her kill two birds with one stone. She needed to keep Jo safely inside the shop for a little while longer. If she could distract her trainee and keep the coast clear for about ten more minutes—

'The windows?' said Jo. 'What about them?'

'Cactuses!' said Milly.

'Eh?'

'Remember a few weeks ago you wanted to buy in a collection of cactuses and carnivorous plants?' she said.

'You hated that idea!' said Jo.

'Change of heart,' said Milly. 'And I want you to design a full window display with them. You can curate your own Jo Burton Collection!'

'Amazing!' said Jo, her eyes lighting up with excitement. 'But... why the change of heart?'

'Those teeth,' said Milly. 'You and all the weirdos who wanted to find them...'

'The kind of weirdos who'd love my grumpy plant collection?' said Jo.

'Exactly,' Milly nodded. 'New clients.'

'Yes!' said Jo with a victorious fist-pump. 'Way to go, toothless best man!'

Milly rolled her eyes. She'd just managed to bring the conversation straight back round to the one subject she was trying to avoid.

'Ooh this is going to be brilliant,' said Jo, skipping towards the windows. 'I'll get a new set of shelving here, and then...'

'And then?' said Milly, cringing slightly as Jo paused to stare through the shop window.

'Milly Rowlands!' she gasped.

'What?' said Milly, doing her best to look curious rather than well and truly horrified.

'Why is there a man doing the walk of shame out of your flat?' said Jo.

'What man?' said Milly.

'That one!' said Jo. 'The one about three feet away - wearing shorts and a tee shirt and *bed hair!*'

'I don't see him,' said Milly, lying through her teeth.

'Him!' said Jo, pointing at Murray.

The man in question had clearly noticed Jo's finger pointing straight at him. He paused and waved at her sheepishly.

'Oh – *that* man!' said Milly with a little smile.

There was no point denying it any longer. Murray was still wearing the same outfit he'd turned up in for their date the day before, and he looked deliciously crumpled. Just the sight of him was doing something strange to her stomach… or maybe that was the vat of ice cream they'd overdosed on the previous night. She'd never be able to look at salted caramel the same way again.

'So,' said Jo, turning her back on Murray to stare at Milly. 'You guys enjoy a sleepover, huh?'

'Shh!' hissed Milly as Murray poked his head inside the shop.

'Erm… you two fancy a coffee?' he said, running a hand through his tousled hair. Milly's knees turned to treacle as she remembered doing that herself just a few hours ago. Their kisses had tasted of chocolate brownies.

'Cappuccino for me, please!' said Jo, taking advantage of the fact that her boss was momentarily tongue-tied.

'Cake?' said Murray.

Jo turned to Milly with wide eyes. 'Marry him.'

Milly smirked as a combination of terror and amusement flitted across Murray's face.

'Don't mind Jo,' she said. 'She thinks she's a comedian.'

'Right…' said Murray, doing the hair thing again.

*Wibble!*

'I'll have the same, please,' said Milly, keen to buy herself a few minutes to get her head together. 'And since you're offering – we like the meringues.'

'We do!' said Jo, nodding with reverence.

'Coming up,' said Murray, smiling and shooting her a wink before ambling off.

'So...' said Jo.

'Yeah,' said Milly, resigned to the fact that she was going to spend the rest of the day getting well and truly grilled.

'You're dating one of the wedding guests?' said Jo.

'Murray was the best man,' said Milly.

'Nope - the best man was short and arsy,' said Jo, shaking her head. 'Your guy saved me from him – so he already gets brownie points.'

'Oh – you must have met Josh,' said Milly as the penny dropped. Jo's message threatening to flob in the best man's hipflask suddenly made sense. She hadn't been talking about Murray at all. 'Murray said he's a bit of a knob – and thoroughly miffed the groom didn't ask him to be best man. He took over after the ambulance came for Murray. His speech knocked years off my life.'

'Sounds like the guy,' said Jo. 'Anyway - back to more interesting things - you slept with the best man?'

'Jo!'

'What?' said Jo. 'Fine. If you want to be all Elizabethan about it... you're being *courted* by the best man?'

'His name's Murray,' said Milly, not really wanting to confirm or deny anything.

'And he's the one who got knocked out by the

bouquet?' said Jo.

'Yep,' said Milly.

'Right,' said Jo. 'So - what's it like kissing someone with missing teeth?'

'He's got all his teeth!' laughed Milly.

'Oh,' said Jo. 'Well, that's disappointing.'

'Not really,' said Milly with a sigh.

'Eww, gross!' said Jo.

'No seriously – all his teeth are still intact.'

'I wasn't talking about the teeth thing,' said Jo. 'You. You've gone all… sweet and melty. It's disturbing!'

Milly let out a snort of amusement.

'So,' said Jo, 'let me get this straight. When you disappeared on Monday - leaving me to fend off the hoards on my lonesome - you were, in fact, abandoning me to chase after a boy?'

'No! Or… maybe… a little bit?' said Milly, suddenly feeling like their roles had been reversed and she was about to get a thorough telling off. 'Sorry?'

'Don't apologise,' said Jo with a shrug. 'It's about time you found someone to fancy.'

'I'm a grown-up, Jo – I don't use words like *fancy*,' she said primly.

'What would you say, then?' said Jo.

Milly tilted her head to think about it. 'Nope, you're right. *Fancy* just about covers it.'

'Ah, young love!' chuckled Jo.

'Hush you,' said Milly. 'Now - go practise your buttonholes!'

# EPILOGUE

## CRUMBLETON TIMES AND ECHO - 25TH JULY

**What's on This Week**

**The Launch of Jo Burton's Grumpy Plant Collection**

Join Jo and Milly at *Milly's Flowers* on Wednesday evening for the grand reveal of their new collection. If prickly, stinky, sticky or just downright terrifying is your thing – grab yourself a Grumpy Plant – and stay for a glass of Bloody Fizz and a Venus Flytrap cupcake while you're there!

**Council Boats – A New Addition and Maintenance**

Some of you will have spotted the snazzy new rowing boat down at Marsh Wharf. Due to a marked increase in the use of the old boat in recent weeks – meaning that keen visiting birdwatchers have not been able to row out in search of the Little Egrets – the council has supplied a brand new boat. The old craft is currently away for maintenance and will be back in action next week.

**A Note From the Museum**

Due to the ongoing search for a new Curator at Crumbleton Museum, all donations are currently on hold apart from on Thursday mornings when Andy Morgan has kindly volunteered to unlock and supervise for half an hour between 9.30am and 10am. Please do not leave donations outside at any other time. Andy would also like to remind everyone that old sofas do not count as historical artefacts.

THE END

## ALSO BY BETH RAIN

**Seabury Series:**

Welcome to Seabury (Seabury Book 1)

Trouble in Seabury (Seabury Book 2)

Christmas in Seabury (Seabury Book 3)

Sandwiches in Seabury (Seabury Book 4)

Secrets in Seabury (Seabury Book 5)

Surprises in Seabury (Seabury Book 6)

Dreams and Ice Creams in Seabury (Seabury Book 7)

Mistakes and Heartbreaks in Seabury (Seabury Book 8)

Laughter and Happy Ever After in Seabury (Seabury Book 9)

A Quiet Life in Seabury (Seabury Book 10)

In A Spin in Seabury (Seabury Book 11)

Living The Dream in Seabury (Seabury Book 12)

A Big Day in Seabury (Seabury Book 13)

Something Borrowed in Seabury (Seabury Book 14)

A Match Made in Seabury (Seabury Book 15)

**Seabury Series Collections:**

Kate's Story: Books 1 - 3

Hattie's Story: Books 4 - 6

Standalones: Books 7 - 9

Lizzie's Story: Books 10 - 12

**Upper Bamton Series:**

Upper Bamton: The Complete Series Collection: Books 1 - 4

**Individual titles:**

A New Arrival in Upper Bamton (Upper Bamton Book 1)

Rainy Days in Upper Bamton (Upper Bamton Book 2)

Hidden Treasures in Upper Bamton (Upper Bamton Book 3)

Time Flies By in Upper Bamton (Upper Bamton Book 4)

**Standalone Books:**

How to be Angry at Christmas

**Crumbleton Series:**

Coming Home to Crumbleton (Crumbleton Book 1)

Flowers Go Flying in Crumbleton (Crumbleton Book 2)

Match Point in Crumbleton (Crumbleton Book 3)

A Very Crumbleton Christmas (Crumbleton Book 4)

**Little Bamton Series:**

Little Bamton: The Complete Series Collection: Books 1 - 5

**Individual titles:**

Christmas Lights and Snowball Fights (Little Bamton Book 1)

Spring Flowers and April Showers (Little Bamton Book 2)

Summer Nights and Pillow Fights (Little Bamton Book 3)

Autumn Cuddles and Muddy Puddles (Little Bamton Book 4)

Christmas Flings and Wedding Rings (Little Bamton Book 5)

**Crumcarey Island Series:**

Crumcarey Island Series Collection: Books 1 - 5

**Individual titles:**

Christmas on Crumcarey (Crumcarey Island Book 1)

All Change on Crumcarey (Crumcarey Island Book 2)

Making Waves on Crumcarey (Crumcarey Island Book 3)

Fool's Gold on Crumcarey (Crumcarey Island Book 4)

A Fresh Start on Crumcarey (Crumcarey Island Book 5)

WRITING AS BEA FOX

What's a Girl To Do? The Complete Series

**Individual titles:**

The Holiday: What's a Girl To Do? (Book 1)

The Wedding: What's a Girl To Do? (Book 2)

The Lookalike: What's a Girl To Do? (Book 3)

The Reunion: What's a Girl To Do? (Book 4)

At Christmas: What's a Girl To Do? (Book 5)

ABOUT THE AUTHOR

Beth Rain has always wanted to be a writer and has been penning adventures for characters ever since she learned to stare into the middle-distance and daydream.

She recently moved to a windswept, Scottish island, and it is a dream come true to spend her days hanging out with Bob – her trusty laptop – scoffing crisps and chocolate while dreaming up swoony love stories for all her imaginary friends.

Beth's writing will always deliver on the happy-ever-afters, so if you need cosy… you're in safe hands!

Visit www.bethrain.com for all the bookish goodness and keep up with all Beth's news by joining her newsletter!

facebook.com/BethRainBooks
twitter.com/bethrainauthor
instagram.com/bethrainauthor

Printed in Great Britain
by Amazon